# SILVER CITY

Ex-army sergeant Pat Flynn and a young Negro called Tobias had come to Silver City to seek their fortune through their combined skills of marksmanship and fist-fighting. All goes to plan until Tobias is given the job of town sheriff, but when the railway enters Silver City its Southern owners' hatred for blacks turns young Tobias into a killing machine. Taking to the hills he rescues a pretty Indian squaw named Nahita from a gang of outlaws. Her village having been wiped out, she and Tobias are two outcasts determined to seek revenge.

# SILVER CITY

*by*

Harold Lamb

**Dales Large Print Books**
Long Preston, North Yorkshire,
BD23 4ND, England.

British Library Cataloguing in Publication Data.

Lamb, Harold
 Silver City.

 A catalogue record of this book is
 available from the British Library

 ISBN   1-84262-464-4 pbk
 ISBN   978-1-84262-464-7 pbk

First published in Great Britain 1994 by Robert Hale Limited

Published in Large Print 2006 by arrangement with
Robert Hale Ltd.

Dales Large Print is an imprint of Library Magna Books Ltd.

Printed and bound in Great Britain by
T.J. (International) Ltd., Cornwall, PL28 8RW

# ONE

The buckboard stopped two miles out of town. The big man pulled on the reins and turned to speak to the blanket-shrouded figure in the back.

'There she is, Tobias, Silver City. Are you still asleep, you big lump? Wake up.' The voice, in a thick Irish brogue, failed to move what was under the cover, so Flynn picked up his rifle and prodded him. A black, curly head poked out of the top of the blanket.

'Yes Sergeant.' The voice spoke with a cultured English accent.

'Silver City, Tobias.' He pointed with the rifle as he spoke. 'And don't call me sergeant. Those days are over.'

The man under the blanket stretched his arms, eased his long legs over the side of the buckboard and stood up to his full height of six foot two inches. George Tobias always reminded him of a big cat, thought Pat Flynn, ex-sergeant of the horse cavalry.

The war between the North and South had been over a few years now. When the South had surrendered, they had stayed on for another couple of years. The talk of fighting Indians had not pleased them, so they had decided to leave and seek their fortune.

Flynn had met Tobias when his platoon had been engaged in a battle with a bunch of Johnny Rebs who had attacked and slaughtered the owner and all the workers of a cotton plantation. Tobias had escaped to Flynn's platoon, where he joined and fought for the North against the South.

The fortune they sought was down there, in Silver City, in what had once been a small town called Tuscany but which had been renamed, once silver had been found in the surrounding hills, and was now a thriving community whose main concerns were cattle and silver.

Next week would see a two-week festival of activities: a competition for riflemen with a $1,000 prize; pistol shooting with an equal amount of prize money and a boxing competition with a grand prize of $5,000 for the supreme champion. Contestants would be chosen on the day of the event and each one would be required to pay a $10 entrance fee.

'Are we going into town or are we camping here?' Tobias asked.

'There's a good spot over there.' Flynn

pointed as he led the way. Trees skirted the lower slope of rising ground, down which tumbled a fresh-water stream. To the right they gave way to encircle a small glade.

'This will do nicely,' said Flynn. 'A ready-made training ground. You'll be able to work out here without any distractions.'

Tobias nodded his agreement. 'I'll get the buckboard, Pat.'

Pat Flynn watched him as he led the horse and buckboard under the cover of the trees. What an athletic build – wide shoulders, slim waist; his feet did not seem to touch the ground as he walked.

Flynn remembered that night when he had come into the camp, with the Johnny Rebs shooting at him. A young, wide-eyed, black youth who had startled them with his impeccable English accent, as he told them of his master's death and the killing of the workers by the Rebs. Flynn's platoon had gone in and shot all of the killers. Nobody was found alive on the plantation. It had belonged to a Philip Tobias, an Englishman who had come to live in America. He had bought his plantation, complete with its slaves and was mollified to find that they expected to take his surname as theirs, now that he was their new master. He found the thought of slavery abhorrent. If they were to take his name then he would treat them like his family. This he did, and over the years they became paid workers, with rights and responsibilities for their own welfare. He made sure that they were well housed and well fed. He treated them fairly and with kindness and was rewarded with good work and prosperity. All his workers were surnamed Tobias and all those born on the plantation since he bought it, were taught English and how to read and write. He saw to that. He had been an English Army officer and had been in many warring situations. He had had his fill of death and carnage and when the American Civil War started he would not take sides or get involved in any way. He just carried on producing cotton. He was a good pistol shot and an excellent boxer and found an eager and skilful pupil in George Tobias. He was a rarity – an educated Negro.

Flynn, an ex-bare-fist fighter from Ireland, had taken him under his wing. It was when they were sitting round the camp-fire one evening swapping yarns that Flynn had mentioned fighting. Tobias told him that Philip Tobias had taught him to box. Flynn had laughed and asked him to show him what he meant by box. Good-naturedly, the rest of the soldiers had formed a circle and watched disbelievingly as Tobias had given Flynn a boxing lesson he had never forgotten.

They had become firm friends and this and their combined skills in shooting and fist-fighting had brought them to the outskirts of Silver City. They had read about the festival and had decided to enter all three competitions – Flynn with his rifle and Tobias with his fists and pistol.

They unloaded the buckboard. Flynn made a rod and went fishing downstream while Tobias put up the tent and made a fire. The bullet sliced into the water making Flynn jump away from the bank as the whine followed behind it. Then a shout, 'Stay where you are,' came from the trees. Tobias, hearing the shot, was now within range and, like Flynn, he froze. Both men remained still, waiting to see who came from the cover.

'Stand up.' It was a female voice. 'Get together, by the water, where I can see you.'

Flynn stood still as Tobias came down to the stream and stood beside him.

The girl stepped from behind a tree and came towards them. Small and slim with her blonde hair tied back, she was dressed in a dark, split riding-skirt, with a white shirt-blouse. Her hat hung, from its thong, behind her and in her hands was a steadily held rifle, pointed fearlessly straight towards them. 'You're trespassing. This is private land.'

'We didn't know it was private land, ma'am,' said Flynn. 'We just want to stop-over for a few days before we go into town for the festival.'

She came closer to the two men, still aiming the rifle. 'You can start packing now and move out.' She followed them the short distance to their camp and stopped a few yards away from the buckboard, watching, as Tobias started to load it up. Flynn asked her if she would accept a rent for the few days they wanted to stay. As she turned to reply Tobias seized his opportunity. She was knocked over by the sack that he had been loading on to the buggy. Before she could recover, Tobias stepped in to snatch the rifle away from her loosened grasp.

Flynn stooped to help her up. 'It's OK. Now don't struggle. We'll be gone as soon as we've packed up.' Tobias handed her the rifle, as two men rode up.

'Hello, Elly. You're not thinking of hiring these two are you? A Negro and an old man? Well now, you must be getting really desperate. My offer still stands. You can marry me or take the money.'

She pointed her rifle at the man who was speaking. 'I'll never marry you, Todd Bates, nor will I sell out. I'd rather die first. Now get off my land.' She cocked the rifle as she spoke. Todd Bates spurred his horse forward, knocking the rifle aside.

'You'll sell by the time I've finished with you.' He stepped down from his horse. Tall, six foot, wide shouldered, with a Navy Colt tied down on his left hip – he reached out to grab Elly. That was when Pat Flynn hit him, knocking him under his horse.

'Hold it. Back off.' The other rider spoke, edging his horse forward, revolver pointing at Flynn. 'Get up Todd,' he told his companion. Todd Bates struggled to his feet and reached for his gun. 'Don't do anything stupid. Your father won't be pleased with this.'

Holstering his gun and remounting, Bates faced Flynn. 'You haven't seen the last of me,' he said as he swung his horse round and set off for Silver City.

Flynn turned to the woman, who was picking up her rifle. 'What was that all about?' he enquired.

'I'm sorry. It seems I've got you into some serious trouble. That was Todd Bates and his partner, Mark Edge, a notorious gun-fighter, who works for Todd's father. Now

11

you have crossed them your stay in Silver City will be endangered.'

Flynn smiled. 'Don't you worry about us. It's you who seems to be in danger. Tell us your problem, ma'am. We may be able to help.'

Elly was more at ease now with Flynn and Tobias. She told them that her husband had been killed by Mark Edge, in a gun-fight in Silver City, in front of so-called witnesses, who had said that it was a fair fight but she knew that her husband had been murdered. The problem had started when they had refused to sell their land and large milk herd to John Bates, Todd's father, who wanted to annex their property. All her hands had left. They were scared off by Mark Edge, who threatened to call them out when they went into town for a drink.

'Do you want to hire two good hands? We don't know much about cattle but I am sure you can teach us. My name's Pat Flynn, ex-US Cavalry and this is Tobias ... and you are–?'

'Elly Morgan,' she replied, 'but you'd be putting your lives at stake.'

Pat Flynn picked up his Winchester rifle, checked it and wiped it clean. He pointed to a tree across the stream. 'Bottom branch,

12

left-hand side.' He raised the rifle to his shoulder. The first shot took off the end of the branch. Four more quick shots shortened the branch further. Every one was a hit. 'Feed us for the time we are here and you have two ranch hands at your service.'

Tobias resumed his task of loading the buggy. Elly Morgan stood, open-mouthed. That was the best rifle shooting she had ever seen. 'But when Mark Edge calls you out he will be close up and it will be pistol work. You won't have a chance with a rifle,' she pointed out.

'We will worry about that when we have to.' Tobias spoke, as he came up to stand by Flynn. His English accent gave Elly Morgan her second shock. 'All ready to go now, Pat.'

Elly Morgan retrieved and mounted her horse and led the way. Tobias sat up alongside Flynn as they followed her the few miles to her compact, neat ranch. The sound of cattle came from the large barn, at the back of the ranch-house. A small bunk-house, on the other side of the barn was to be their living quarters. As they rounded the back of the ranch-house they saw that further buildings, housing the stables, stores and equipment, as well as their sleeping quarters, enclosed a large cobbled courtyard.

'Unload your stuff and I'll go see about some grub,' Elly said as she dismounted from her horse. 'Mano,' she called, in the direction of the barn.

'*Si*, Miss Elly,' came the reply as an old Mexican came out of the barn, carrying a pail of milk. He stopped on seeing a white man and a Negro sitting alongside one another on the buckboard. 'Miss Elly…' he began, then stood, mouth agape, pointing. Elly laughed at his confusion.

'Meet our new hired help, Mano. Show them where to stable their horse and buggy and help them settle in to the bunk-house. Then we will eat, before you show them how to milk the cows.' She smiled at him and then continued, 'That's Tobias, unloading the buggy and this here is Mr Flynn.' With that she returned to the house to supervise their meal and left the three men to get acquainted. Mano was pleased to have company in the bunk-house again though he was a little nonplussed by the relationship between the two men and the strange lingo of the Negro. It did not take long for them to settle in. Tobias put on a pair of moccasins and, taking a skipping rope from his pack, proceeded to skip in a corner of the bunk-house. After watching him warm up Flynn took out his watch and shouted, 'fifteen minutes.'

An OK from the big Negro was the only answer. Mano sat on his bunk watching and wondering. Flynn smiled. 'How long will grub be?'

'Miss Elly will shout,' answered Mano, his eyes glued to the exercising Tobias, watching the speed of the rope as it whirled round and the dexterity of the Negro crossing his hands, jumping up, the rope a blur, spinning twice as he hung in mid-air. Then his knees were up under his chin, his timing perfect, his breathing deep and steady. Flynn's voice broke the sound of the pat-pat-patter of the rope hitting the floor. 'Two minutes.'

The speed increased and sweat appeared on Tobias's brow. 'Time.' The watch was put away. Then the shadow boxing began. Left foot forward, jab, elbows tucked in, Flynn's voice calling out as the big Negro moved about following instructions. Mano watched – eyes transfixed.

'Time. Outside now, Tobias.' Mano followed them outside, wondering what was to happen next. Flynn found a large rock and passed it to Tobias, who took it effortlessly. Push-ups. Push-outs. Up, down. Out, in. Tobias followed Flynn's instructions.

15

'Grub up.' Elly Morgan's shout ended the workout. Flynn set to work on Tobias, rubbing, kneading and massaging before wiping him dry. Mano saw how closely they worked together. He was amazed by it all.

They sat at the table, eating, Tobias quiet as usual, knife and fork busy, Flynn asking what chores Elly wanted them to do before they retired.

'Mano will take you to the barn while I clear this lot away. The late milking has to be done. I will be out shortly.'

After cleaning the pots and dishes, she entered the barn to find Flynn and Tobias working well under Mano's expert supervision. Soon she was helping. Between the four of them the milking and other chores were quickly completed. Elly Morgan showed them over the spread. As well as the milk herd, she had some first-class beef cattle. There was no shortage of water on the ranch and the pond was kept full by an underwater spring. Flynn could see that it was a little gold mine. It was no wonder that John Bates wanted it.

'You still haven't told me what you are both here for,' said Elly Morgan as they made their way back towards the main buildings.

'He's here to win the boxing tournament,'

16

explained Flynn, 'and he might also win the pistol-shooting contest. Me, I hope to win the rifle shooting.'

'You have to qualify for each of the shooting contests,' said Elly. 'I've seen you shoot but Mr Tobias will be up against Mark Edge and he doesn't miss.' Tobias went into the bunk-house and came out carrying a parcel from which he took a holstered Colt and opening the belt, he took out the bullets from the leather clip and loaded the gun. Then he bent down and picked up five small pebbles, which he placed along the fence, a foot apart. Walking fifteen paces, he turned. Up came his arm in a slow, easy movement. Five shots rang out. Five pebbles leapt off the top of the fence.

Flynn looked at Elly Morgan. 'And he fights much better.'

'What if Mark Edge was to call one of you out? I've seen him kill. He likes doing it.'

Tobias put on his gun belt and came over to stand in front of Elly Morgan. In his best English accent he said, 'Clap your hands, please. Any time you are ready.' His right hand was poised over his gun.

Elly Morgan looked over at Flynn. 'What does he want me to do?'

'Like he says ma'am, clap your hands – in

front of him – as quick as you can, when you're ready.'

Elly stood in front of Tobias. The size of him made her feel weak. She could feel the power of him. She clapped her hands. He had not moved. If he had, she had not seen him. His gun was between her palms. Her hands dropped to her sides. The pistol was put back in its holster.

'Do it faster,' Flynn said.

She obliged, this time with more speed. The gun still found its way between her palms. Tobias put his pistol away and took off his gun belt. As he was wrapping it up, a big, solid man rode up to the ranch-house. Ignoring the company he approached Elly Morgan, who met him with, 'What do you want, John Bates? You're not welcome here.'

Alerted by the name, Flynn moved closer to Elly.

'Has Todd been here?' There was no respect in his voice. Heavy leaden eyes, set in a thick-jowled, unsmiling face, glanced at Flynn and Tobias.

'You're not welcome here, Miss Elly said.' Tobias spoke, stepping forward to stand by Bates's horse.

'I don't speak to Negroes.' John Bates lashed out at Tobias with his right foot.

18

Tobias grabbed it and, twisting, threw the rancher off the back of his horse. Bates rolled on to his side and reached for his gun as Tobias closed in. Flynn's rifle came up and fired as the gun in Bates's hand levelled at Tobias. The pistol flew out of the rancher's hand as Tobias reached down and grabbed him by his shirt. He pulled him, effortlessly, to his feet and delivered a punch, so powerful, that Bates bounced back on to the ground, where he lay still.

Mano picked up a bucket, went to the horse-trough, filled it with water and sluiced it over the recumbent rancher, who coughed and spluttered as he tried to get up. Tobias unceremoniously hauled him to his feet. He jammed the rancher's hat on to his head, retrieved and holstered his gun and pushed him towards his horse.

'Don't come back unless you are invited,' he quietly advised; 'and if you pull a gun on me again I'll kill you.'

Bates, a big man, suddenly felt inadequate in the black man's presence. He climbed, unsteadily, aboard his horse and rode away, without so much as a glance back. Tobias picked up his gun and belt and walked to the bunk-house without a word.

Elly watched him go. 'Is he always that

quiet?' Flynn nodded. 'What did he say to John Bates?' she enquired.

'Probably told him to stay away, if I know Tobias.' Flynn walked towards the bunkhouse, turning in the doorway to wish her and Mano goodnight.

'I don't know what we have taken on, Mano, but suddenly I feel very safe. Goodnight.'

Mano checked and secured the outbuildings before turning in. He was glad to find the new hands already settled down for the night; that meant a good, early start in the morning.

## TWO

Next day, once the morning chores were out of the way, Flynn and Tobias went into Silver City, riding saddle horses loaned to them by Elly. They passed tents camped outside of the city boundaries. It certainly was a thriving community. Either side of the main street, saloons were busy selling beer. The shops and eating-houses were doing just as well. The mayor's office came into sight. Posters advertised the forthcoming events and directed the contestants inside to register and pay their entrance fees. As they entered the office two other men, dressed in city suits, came out. Flynn stood to one side to let them pass. One was a huge man, in contrast to the other who was small and slight of build. Flynn watched them leave with interest.

'That's one to watch. It's Joe Burke, one of the best fighters around, and his backer, Barney O'Rourke.'

Tobias shrugged his massive shoulders. 'He looks a bit old to be a threat.'

'Don't let that fool you. I saw him years ago. He's cagey and can be very dirty,' was Flynn's cautionary reply.

They entered the main office. A short, bald-headed clerk was busy writing in a ledger. He glanced up. 'State which competition you wish to enter. Pay your fee now and see if you are good enough on the day to qualify.' The clerk adjusted his spectacles as he spoke. Flynn signed for the rifle shooting, Tobias for the boxing and the pistol shooting. As he signed George Tobias in bold letters, the clerk looked on in astonishment, at witnessing a Negro being able to write.

They paid their fees and left the office to explore the city. Much work was being done.

Buildings, both domestic and business, were being erected and on the corner of Main Street a theatre was nearing completion. After walking round Silver City, they returned to their horses, mounted up and took the road leading back to Elly Morgan's ranch. Three miles out of Silver City, five riders approached them: Todd Bates and Mark Edge were in the lead. Flynn stopped, pulling his Winchester from its holster. Tobias opened his saddle-bag. They split up, one on each side of the trail, as the five riders drew closer. Flynn could see that three of them were just cattle hands. They were very nervous. He could tell that by the anxious looks on their faces. If there was going to be any trouble it would be the two in the front who would be the most dangerous. Turning to Tobias, Flynn said, 'Take the one nearest to you,' and started forward.

Mark Edge turned to Todd Bates. 'They're splitting up. We could be in trouble. Don't do anything unless we can take them both.'

'The black man isn't wearing a gun,' Bates replied.

Flynn rode with the rifle, across his horse's neck, pointing towards Bates, who was the nearest to him. Edge was watching Tobias, who was riding with his hand trailing down by the right-hand side of his saddle, slightly to the rear, as if he was adjusting his saddle-bag. Flynn spoke as they got nearer. 'Good afternoon, gentlemen. Did your father find you, yesterday? He seemed to have lost his way, when we saw him.'

The five stopped. The horses mingled. The three ranch hands, wishing to stay clear of Edge and Bates, pulled their horses back, watching Flynn, who was now pointing his rifle in Bates's direction. Bates's hand dropped to his pistol.

'If you pull it, you won't fire it.' Flynn's finger was now on his rifle trigger. 'And if Edge wants to try it, perhaps he will be luckier than your father.' Edge was watching Tobias as he eased his horse closer towards him. His hand was now in his saddle-bag. Edge could sense the danger of him. He slowly and carefully placed both his hands where they could be seen by both Tobias and Flynn.

'It seems that you have the drop on us this time.' He put a restraining hand on Bates's gun hand. 'Maybe next time, gentlemen.'

He found it hard not to show his anger as he spurred his horse forward, away from Flynn's menacing rifle and whatever was in the black man's saddle-bag. Flynn turned to watch them ride away, then he replaced his rifle in its saddle holster. Tobias's hand came out of his saddle-bag clutching two apples. He threw one to Flynn and started eating the other as he sent his horse away with Flynn shouting abuse at him. He did not catch up with him till they got back to the ranch.

'What was in the saddle-bag besides apples?' Flynn asked as he snatched the bag out of Tobias's hands. He plunged his hand into the bag and rummaged round. Finding nothing he threw the bag back at him. 'One day, Tobias, you are going to get us both killed.'

'Me? You started it, Pat,' was the calm reminder, as Flynn followed Tobias into the bunk-house. 'That could have turned nasty back there. The next time we meet could be our last,' Tobias reflected as he stripped off and put on his training gear. He took out his skipping rope and started to skip. 'I've decided to wear my gun all the time,' he said, as the rope whirred round. 'As much as I don't want to, I'm going to have to tote it. They thought I had a gun in my saddle-bag. The bluff fooled them today. Next time we may not be so lucky.' Flynn shook his head at the coolness of his young friend.

'You know that if you wear it you'll be asking for Edge to call you out?'

Tobias nodded and trapped the rope under his foot. 'And then I will kill him,' he said, calmly, before returning to his training and speeding up his footwork.

Once the skipping exercises were completed, they went to the barn to look for Mano to ask him to time a sparring session. Flynn patiently showed him how to use the watch to give them three minutes of sparring, then one minute's rest. Satisfied that Mano understood what was required of him, Flynn stripped off his shirt. Mano could see by his well-muscled body and the way he moved around that Flynn was fit and looked after himself. Both men wore gloves. After loosening up Flynn told Mano they were ready.

'Time,' the Mexican called out. Both men swapped punches. Pat Flynn, the more experienced of the two, tried every trick he could think of to catch Tobias off-guard. Slipping punches, moving inside and holding, dropping his head to try to catch Tobias with head butts, all proved to no avail. Tobias's speed of punch, his balance and footwork was something to behold. Mano called time. Flynn spoke to Tobias between rounds, telling him and showing him how to react if he was gouged; what to do if he was heeled down his shin, and much more. So it went on, both men swapping punches, Mano calling time and providing them with drinks between rounds. After ten rounds Flynn told Tobias that he was ready and took a towel and began to rub him down. Mano looked on. The big, black muscled body oozed tremendous strength. No one would ever be able to beat this one, Mano thought.

A noise at the door drew the men's attention. Elly stood there. 'How long have you been there?' It was Flynn, as usual, doing the asking.

'Long enough,' she replied. 'I hope you've some energy left for the evening milking and the rest of the chores.' She looked at Tobias. Her eyes hid the feelings she felt. How long had it been since her husband had died? She turned and went outside, leaving the men to get on with their work.

The following week saw the start of the festivities. Tobias and Flynn entered the city. Tobias wore his Navy Colt, tied down low on his right hip. Flynn, Coltless, his rifle in its saddle-holster. Elly and Mano promised to follow them in later, once the ranch chores were done. Bill Campbell, the famous buffalo hunter and Indian fighter, was there when Pat Flynn arrived for the elimination heats of the rifle-shooting contest. A great fuss was made when Campbell came up to shoot. Each contestant was to fire at a swinging target, at fifty feet, using six shots. The highest-scoring ten contestants were to go through to the final, later on in the week. Three local men had already competed. The most scored so far was four hits, so one had high hopes of getting through.

Altogether thirty contestants had paid to enter. Campbell was the first to hit six from six, using his massive buffalo gun. Three other contestants, including Todd Bates, hit five. Pat Flynn came after Bates. Standing left foot forward, his Winchester came to his shoulder. Taking aim he fired off his first shot, which was a direct hit. Five more shots followed. Five more hits. The crowd applauded Flynn's shooting. Five more contestants followed scoring fours and fives and, when all the entrants had competed, the ten highest scores were sorted out and the list of names was posted.

Then came the pistol shooting, with the contestants aiming, from fifty feet, at six standing glass targets. They presented difficult targets being three inches in width. A number of locals had fired off at the targets and their scores reflected the degree of difficulty and the skill required, in this competition.

Bill Marsden, Silver City's marshal, had been a well-known gunman in his youth, but he was slowing down as he got older. He was the first to hit five of the six targets. Mark Edge equalled his score. When George Tobias was called out, there were gasps and mutterings from the crowd. One or two made detrimental comments about him to the amusement of those around them. Tobias's face was immobile as he stepped forward.

'Are you Tobias?' one of the judges asked. 'A Negro shooter?'

'Does it matter who, or what, I am?' Tobias took his gun from his holster, checked it and put it back. He faced the targets, paused, then drew his gun. The right arm rose. Five shots: five glasses exploded. The arm rose a fraction. Tobias missed deliberately. 'Five hits gets me through, sir?' The question was asked in his best English accent and the emphasis was on the *sir*. The judge nodded. No one acknowledged Tobias's skill but by their silence, the crowd told him what he already knew. His chances of winning were as good as anyone else's there.

Later on, in the new theatre, the eliminating heats of the heavyweight boxing contest were staged. A large crowd had gathered for the fights. Seven men had entered – four locals and the three outsiders – Tobias, Burke and Hoch. Of the three, Joe Burke was the only one the crowd had heard of. He was in the first bout, against a local miner, who was well known for his bar-room brawls. A lot of the silver miners were backing him. Burke was introduced to the expectant crowd. A mixed reception welcomed him. Then the local miner, a huge man named Wallace, was cheered as he entered the ring, waving to the crowd at the reception he was given. A light glove was being used and a rough fight was anticipated between Burke and Wallace. And a rough fight it was. Wallace mixed it with Burke from the first round. It was the guile and skill of Burke that saved him, time and time again. A big, strong man was Wallace. He walked forward, swinging punches, but Burke slipped most of them. During the third round, Burke's fitness began to tell. He was catching Wallace now and, as he lunged forward, a right uppercut followed by a left hook put Wallace down and out.

The next contest was between two locals who were pretty well matched. A wild swing from one of them caused a big cut over his opponent's eye and so ended the fight. The winner was to fight Burke. The remaining contestant got a bye. He was to fight the winner of the Tobias-Hoch bout. The third contest was announced. Tobias was to fight against the Dutchman, Curt Hoch, from San Francisco, a seaman with a reputation as a hard puncher, with boxing skills he had learned from his travels round the world. The first into the ring was Tobias. The crowd murmured amongst themselves at the size of him, his muscles rippling as he went through his loosening-up exercises. Flynn was rubbing him, talking, giving instructions. A cheer went up as Hoch appeared and made his way to the ring. A big, blond-haired man, handsome with wide shoulders and not an ounce of fat on him. Flynn looked at him. He could see he was a fit man. Ducking under the rope, Hoch waved to the crowd.

As they were introduced by the MC both men eyed each other, looking for weaknesses. Tobias's face was expressionless. Hoch sensed a feeling in the pit of his stomach. Was it fear or nerves? He did not like what he saw. Tobias noted the slight flicker of fear and Flynn's last instruction was to go straight at him and take him out with a left and right.

'Time,' the timekeeper called. Hoch went

out to meet Tobias. He was met by a straight left. Then a right came from nowhere. Then everything went black and he remembered nothing else until he was being splashed with water and smelling salts were being put under his nose by his second. He was still lying in his corner and the referee was raising Tobias's hand. The crowd could not believe what they had seen. Joe Burke, who had been at the ringside witnessing the power and speed of Tobias's punches, knew then that the final contest, to be held in a few days' time, would be between himself and the Negro.

Unable to find Elly and Mano, Flynn and Tobias went back to the ranch where they told them of the day's events. They were overjoyed at the results. Both had intended to go into town but the work had taken them longer than they had thought. Elly was determined to make it for the shooting finals but she did not want to watch the boxing.

The milking and the chores were completed early on the day of the finals and then all four of them went off to Silver City. There seemed to be more people than ever in town for the festivities. Much of the talk was about the contestants, especially the big pistolero, Mark Edge and marshal Bill

Marsden in the pistol-shooting and Bill Campbell and Pat Flynn in the rifle shoot-out. Money was being laid on them all.

After a meal they all went to the designated area where Flynn joined the other nine finalists. They were allowed ten shots each, to be done in two sets of five at swinging targets. Three of them scored maximum points – Todd Bates, Bill Campbell and Pat Flynn. Smaller targets were introduced for the three finalists. Todd Bates stepped up and the targets were set in motion. He had four hits from his first five shots. Flynn followed, scoring five out of five. Bill Campbell scored four from five. The three had a five-minute break and then returned for the final round. Bates, first again, was a man showing anger, who this time scored three out of five. Flynn, calm, left foot forward, lifting his rifle up to his shoulder fired five true shots. Campbell declined to shoot. He just came forward and shook hands with Flynn, telling him that his was the best rifle shooting he had seen for a long time. Todd Bates turned his back and walked away with his father and the rest of his crew, which included Mark Edge.

Elly, with Mano and Tobias, congratulated Flynn, who had been declared the winner and been presented with the $1,000 prize money. Other events were in progress and they went off to watch them. They had time to spare as the pistol shooting was not due to start till later on in the day. Mano walked ahead with Flynn, leaving Elly to talk with Tobias.

'You and Pat Flynn get on very well, don't you?'

Tobias nodded. 'He looked after me when I joined his company, during the war with the South. We have been together ever since then.'

'But where do you come from?' Elly enquired of him.

'I was born on a plantation, owned by Philip Tobias, who brought me up as a son and taught me all I know.'

'What happened? Why did you leave?' she persisted.

Tobias told her of the raid and the ensuing massacre, of his escape and his meeting with Pat Flynn. 'Flynn is like a father to me, now. It's funny. I have had two fathers and both have been white.'

Elly took his arm, as they walked along, quite oblivious to the stares of the passers-by. Todd Bates came into view, with his father and Mark Edge.

'So it's black men you like now, is it?' Bates snarled, as he approached them. Tobias stepped forward in a threatening manner. Mark Edge's right hand went to his hip, caressing his gun.

Flynn was between them in a flash. 'If it's trouble you're after, I can give you all you want, me laddo.' He grabbed Bates by the coat lapels. 'I've beaten you once today and if you want another hiding I can give it to you, now.' Bates struggled to free himself from Flynn's grip but found that he could not. Mark Edge stood to one side, his hand on his gun. Flynn looked at him. 'Well, go on, Edge, draw. He has hidden behind you for a long time. Let me tell you, if you draw you will have to shoot one of us.' He looked at Tobias as he added, 'But first let's see how good Bates is.' With that he hit Bates, knocking him to the ground. Edge drew his gun but it had not cleared his holster when Tobias hit him behind his ear, knocking him off balance. His gun fell from his hand as he went down.

Elly picked it up and pointed it at Todd Bates and his father. 'Stop or I will shoot. Now pick him up.' She pointed at Edge as she spoke. 'Now get.'

The two Bates helped Mark Edge to his

feet. 'Tell him I will leave his gun at the pistol shooting, later.' With that she walked away, still holding the gun.

A big crowd had gathered for the pistol shooting. The word had got round town of the trouble between Elly Morgan's ranch hands and Todd Bates. Knowing Mark Edge, they expected more trouble after the contest. Bill Marsden, the town marshal, had talked to Bates and Edge, warning them that he did not want any shooting in his town that day to mar the proceedings.

The pistol shooting started off amidst a tense atmosphere. Mark Edge had arrived minus his gun, which caused a titter in the crowd till he reclaimed it. Tobias was first to shoot followed by Edge, then Marsden. Tobias hit six glass targets from six shots as did Edge and Marsden. None of the other finalists could equal their score. The distance was increased by ten feet. The three finalists were instructed to take ten shots, in two sets of five, in the same sequence, Tobias leading with Marsden bringing up the rear. The crowd went silent. Tobias stepped forward; his pistol came up. Five shots: five balls exploded. Mark Edge came next, with a confident smirk on his face. His five shots saw four glass balls go down. A curse exploded from his twisted lips. Marsden stepped up next. Slow, but with a steady arm, he had had a lot of experience at pistol shooting. His stance was easy as he aimed and fired at the distant targets. Five shots rang out and all the balls exploded. A big cheer rang out from the crowd for the popular marshal. Tobias took up his position for the final round. Raising his gun he fired off the five shots and five targets exploded bringing his score to ten out of ten. This time the crowd applauded. They knew what good shooting was and they showed their appreciation. Mark Edge was next. Slower this time. Five shots: five hits, making his total nine from ten. The crowd waited with baited breath as Bill Marsden took up his stance. Slow and steady he took aim. Five targets glistened in the sunlight; five shots rang out; all direct hits. The crowd let out a triumphant whoop. It was a tie between Tobias and Marsden. Mark Edge left the arena, unnoticed, in a foul temper, followed by his employers, John and Todd Bates.

The judges called Tobias and the marshal together and asked them if they wanted to share the prize money or have a shoot-out to decide the outright winner. Tobias looked at the marshal, who said, 'Well, we could both use the money so we will share it.' He shook hands with Tobias and turning to the judges he grinned. 'However, I'm sure curious as to who really is the fastest, so if someone could time us, how about setting up five more balls for each of us in turn?' Interest was aroused as the conversation was relayed through the crowd.

A stop-watch was provided by one of the judges. 'Who is going first?' he asked the two men. Marsden said that he should, as it was his idea. Once again the five glass targets were set up. It took Marsden six seconds to draw and fire, hitting four of the targets. He shook his head and grinned at Tobias, 'Show them what you can do, son. Don't miss any, now.'

Tobias nodded. He stood poised, still as a statue, focusing on the glittering targets. He took a deep breath, his gun leapt into his hand. Five shots saw all the targets disintegrate, as one. The judge looked at his stop-watch. 'Four seconds,' he announced. No one clapped or cheered until Marsden gripped Tobias's hand and shook it and then the applause rang out.

Meanwhile, Todd Bates and Mark Edge were in a bar, drowning their sorrows and swearing revenge on Pat Flynn and George Tobias.

Later that evening Elly and Mano went back to the ranch, leaving Flynn and Tobias to prepare for the night's boxing contest. Arriving at the theatre, they were told that both Tobias's opponent and Burke's had pulled out of the fight, so it was decided to bring the final contest forward. The word spread quickly round Silver City that the final was to be in two hours' time. Soon a massive crowd filled the theatre to see Tobias and Joe Burke fight it out. Flynn rested Tobias, watching over him as he slept for an hour. The excitement of winning the shooting contest had eased off now but Flynn wondered how Tobias managed to keep so cool. He recalled how, even when they were under fire in the war, Tobias had never shown any sign of nerves and he knew that tonight, against Burke, he would be just as cool. There was greater danger awaiting him in Silver City, from Mark Edge and Todd Bates, than from his boxing opponent. Flynn woke Tobias and started to work on him with loosening-up exercises and massage and soon had him ready for action.

'I won't let you down, Pat. When we get this fight over we should have enough for a nice spread, somewhere.'

'Burke won't be easy, son. It could be rough for you. He can be dirty if he knows he's losing. I've seen him in action, in Chicago. Don't let him get you in a corner. Box him. Stay in the middle of the ring. If you hit him with a clean punch he will go.'

Tobias nodded. 'I'm ready, Sergeant. Come on.'

Flynn put the towel around his neck and followed him into the theatre. The crowd roared as he appeared on the stage, where the ring was situated. Joe Burke was already in the ring. Flynn took the gloves from the referee, inspected them and started to put them on Tobias. Scott Brady was a referee with a lot of experience behind him. He had asked the town marshal to be the time-keeper. That way everything would be done honestly. Brady called the two fighters together and told them the conditions of the fight – ten rounds, each of three minutes' duration with a one-minute break between rounds. If a contestant did not come up for a round and the bell sounded they were the loser. 'And don't hit below the belt,' was his parting comment as both men returned to their respective corners, to await the bell.

'Time.' The bell sounded.

Burke came across the ring to try and catch Tobias in his corner but Flynn had warned Tobias and he followed instructions. Slipping away to one side, he came back, well balanced, as Burke turned to face him. Tobias's left jab met him. Knocked back into the corner, Burke covered up hoping to lure his opponent into him but he found Tobias standing-off, jabbing with his left, trying to open him up. Burke lunged forward, grabbing at Tobias. A right uppercut met him, then a left hook. He found himself on the floor. The referee was standing over him. The crowd was roaring. At the count of 'Seven,' he was up, looking at Tobias.

This time he showed caution moving around – crouched – making himself a smaller target to hit, slipping the punches being thrown by Tobias. The speed of the punches made it difficult. The jabs kept finding his face. His left eye was starting to swell already. The bell ended the first round.

At the start of the second, Tobias was across the ring to meet him. He staggered as the punch hit him, then he moved in close, hoping to hold on whilst his head cleared. His head caught Tobias on the bridge of his nose. Then he turned, putting Tobias between himself and the referee, his right glove punching between his opponent's legs. Tobias went down, knowing that Burke had deliberately tried to cripple him. He stayed down. His nose ached but the blow in his crotch could have done him some harm if he had not been going backwards. He was angry with himself at being caught by such a crude move. The referee had counted to six. Tobias was up. Flynn was looking over with concern. When Tobias nodded, he knew things were OK. Burke moved in, full of confidence. A one-two, then a left hook stopped him in his tracks. A following straight right knocked him into his corner and before he could hit the floor a left hook keeled him awkwardly on to his right shoulder. When he came round the pain in it, as he was being picked up, made him wince. It was then that he knew that it was dislocated.

Tobias came over to say how sorry he was and to shake hands. Burke looked at him. What the hell makes this man tick? he thought. His hand was gripped and shaken – the pain from his shoulder making him shout out. The referee was shouting for a doctor as Tobias was bowing to the applause of the crowd. Pat Flynn was in the ring with him, fussing over him, wiping his face, looking at his nose for any damage. Tobias put his arm round Flynn.

'I'm all right Pat. No serious damage.' He raised Flynn's hand as he spoke, both men acknowledging the applause of the crowd. Into the ring climbed the marshal to congratulate the winner and his manager.

'Well done. Well done.' He directed his attention to Tobias. 'You handle yourself very well for a young feller.' He turned to Flynn. 'I want to talk to you two later, when you are ready. I'll be in the Red Garter saloon.'

Flynn nodded. 'All right. Come on, Tobias.' He escorted the young Negro from the stage to the changing-room with the roar of the crowd's applause ringing in their ears. He attended to Tobias in his usual efficient way, rubbing him down and then drying him off. Whilst Tobias dressed, Flynn told him about what the marshal had said.

'What do you think he wants?' queried Tobias.

'Don't know, but we can find out,' Flynn replied laconically. Tobias strapped on his gun belt. Flynn looked surprised. 'Are you expecting trouble?'

Tobias tied his gun down. 'There's nothing like being prepared.'

Flynn picked up his rifle, opened it and filled the chamber with bullets. They left the theatre – two big men – not looking for trouble, but if any came their way they would be ready to deal with it. They entered the noisy Red Garter saloon. A piano played somewhere amongst the crowd of dancers and drinkers. Bill Marsden was at the bar with Campbell, the old buffalo hunter. When they saw Tobias and Flynn enter the marshal waved them over. People made way for them at the bar. After quenching his thirst, Flynn asked the marshal what he wanted them for. The marshal put down his drink.

'Well, you have seen the size of Silver City and it's getting bigger every day. Even when the silver runs out it will still be a thriving cattle town and there's talk of the railway coming this way.' He paused for a drink before going on. 'I need two deputies. Men I can trust. I'd like you and Tobias. I've asked Campbell but he says he's too old and anyway, while there's buffalo about, he won't settle in any town for a length of time.' Campbell nodded in agreement.

Flynn's reply came after a pause. 'Well, I promised Tobias if we won enough money I would go into partnership with him and get ourselves a spread somewhere and I won't go back on my word.' They looked to Tobias for his reaction.

'Do you have to know our answer now or can we give it some thought?'

'Let me know in a few days,' the marshal said, ordering more drinks. Tobias declined but Flynn agreed to just one more before they left. Passing the drinks over, the marshal noticed Todd Bates come in with Mark Edge. Both stood by the doors, looking round until they spotted Flynn and Tobias. Todd Bates pointed them out and Edge moved towards them, stopping at the bar where the drinkers, knowing of his reputation as a fast gun, hastily made room for him. No one wanted to fall foul of his temper. He bought himself a drink and turned in the direction of Flynn and Tobias.

'I didn't know you served niggers in here, bartender.' With that, he spat his drink on to the floor. 'It's enough to turn your beer off.' He turned and put his beer back on the bar. The piano stopped playing. Couples on the floor moved away to one side – away from Tobias, who was ignoring Edge till Bill Marsden turned to the gunman, telling him to mind his tongue and not to cause any trouble.

'Is the nigger hiding behind you now, Marshal?' The sneer as he spoke brought Flynn's rifle up in line with his stomach.

Tobias knocked it down.

'No, Pat. Marshal.' His hand rested on Marsden's shoulder, easing him to one side. 'Let's get it over with.' Edge stepped back as Tobias faced him. 'When you're ready.' Tobias spoke, no sign of fear, his right hand dropping to his gun. Edge looked at him. Tobias stepped closer. 'When you are ready ... to die.'

Edge felt fear for the first time in his life. Tobias moved even closer. He could feel his breath on his face. His hand went to his gun. It stopped there. Tobias's hand came up. His gun jabbed Edge in the chest. Then he pulled the trigger. Mark Edge still had his gun in his holster when he hit the floor, a large hole in his chest pumping blood.

'Tobias,' Flynn shouted. Tobias heard Flynn's rifle explode behind him. He turned to his left side to see Todd Bates dropping his gun to the floor, with a hole between his eyes which were staring sightless at Tobias. Todd Bates's body hit the floor with a thud to lie still alongside Mark Edge. Their killing days were over. Tobias turned and thanked Pat Flynn then he looked to the marshal for his reaction to the shootings. He was a bit shaken. The speed and accuracy of the shoot had amazed him. He knew that with these two on his side, to keep order, Silver City would soon become a law-abiding and prosperous place.

The two bodies were removed to the undertaker's on the marshal's orders and things soon got back to normal.

Flynn and Tobias made their way back to the ranch. As they passed the ranch-house, the door opened. Elly was silhouetted in the doorway.

'Everything all right?' she enquired.

Flynn knew she would not rest until she had satisfied her curiosity as to whether Tobias had won the boxing match or not. He stopped. Tobias halted alongside, and touched his hat.

'Evening, ma'am. Things worked out all right. Tobias won. Nothing happened that won't wait till morning. If you'll excuse us now we won't keep you up late.' Both men bid her good-night. Letting the horses loose, after unsaddling and rubbing them down, they made their way to the bunk-house. Following Flynn, Tobias turned to look over to the house. Elly was still there, looking towards him as he went in and closed the door behind him.

Flynn took his arm as he passed his bunk. 'You had to kill him, son.'

Tobias stopped. 'I know, Pat. The trouble is I wanted to.' He went to his bunk, took off his gun, cleaned it and put it away. Flynn wondered if he would put it on again. Mano's snoring made him realize how tired he was. Undressing, he climbed into his bunk and was soon fast asleep. Tobias lay awake for a while thinking of Elly silhouetted in the doorway.

Next morning Mano was first up, making just enough noise to wake the two friends. Flynn woke first and greeted the Mexican. Tobias rose, and stretched his huge body. Mano looked at him, searching for any cuts or swellings and, not seeing any, he asked how the fight had gone. Tobias told him, bringing a broad grin of pleasure to the old Mexican's face. The three of them got dressed and went about their chores and the early milking. After they had finished, Elly sounded the breakfast gong. Their conversation was about the previous day's activities. When breakfast was finished, Tobias started to tell them what had happened in town. He mentioned the job offer from the marshal, then stopped when he saw the look of disappointment on her face.

'You're not leaving here, are you?' she began. Flynn butted in when he saw how uncomfortable Tobias was getting.

'No, we're not,' he assured her and then went on to tell her about the shootings in the Red Garter saloon. Mano dropped his coffee cup on the table in surprise.

'You killed them both?' Elly gasped. 'Both of them? My God, John Bates will be round here as soon as he finds out.'

'He must know by now,' was Tobias's reply. The clatter of hooves outside brought them all up from the table. Elly was first to the door to see John Bates dismounting with two of his ranch hands in attendance. Flynn pushed his way to the front. Bates stopped when he saw him.

'I hope you have not come here to cause trouble.'

'I'm not armed,' answered Bates, holding his hands out in front of him. 'I heard about last night in town – how the killing came about. I'm not blaming you two. I'm as much to blame as you are for allowing things to get out of hand. I'm leaving the area. Moving out. Selling up as soon as I can get a buyer. I just thought you should know.' With that he turned and mounted his horse.

'Mr Bates.' Tobias stepped forward. 'I would like to say how sorry I am.' He extended his hand but the hurt in Bates's

48

eyes caused him to withdraw it.

'How much would you be wanting for your spread?' Flynn enquired.

'If you're interested in buying, we can go to the bank and arrange an agreement now.'

Elly stepped forward and gripped Flynn's arm. 'You two ... as neighbours?'

'Why not? I promised him a spread.' Pat Flynn walked over to where his horse was. 'We could be partners if you can agree something with Tobias while I'm away in town, sorting out the sale.'

He mounted his horse and rode off to Silver City with John Bates.

# THREE

Pat Flynn rode into Silver City with John Bates and his cowhands. The more he saw of Silver City the more he liked it. With silver pouring in and abundant natural grazing for cattle it was a town with great prospects, as long as the crooked element could be kept out. They had a top lawman in Bill Marsden, ageing now but still fast enough to control the unruly element and if Pat and Tobias took up his offer of becoming deputies the future looked promising. Pat Flynn spotted Marshal Marsden, who came over to meet them as they dismounted alongside the bank.

'Morning Flynn,' the marshal spoke, eyeing Bates, who was scowling at him, 'Have you come in for the festivities or have you come in to collect the prize money that you won?'

Flynn did not answer immediately. He could feel the tension between the two men. Marsden stared back at Bates, wondering whether or not the big rancher was thinking of revenge for his son's death at the hands of Flynn and Tobias.

'I haven't come in looking for revenge, Marsden,' growled Bates. 'I'm selling up to Flynn and that damned nigger-friend of his and moving out. But let me tell you this, if you had done your job properly there wouldn't have been no killing.'

'Your boy got what he asked for last night, Bates, along with Mark Edge.'

Turning his back on the marshal, John Bates went into the bank with Pat Flynn walking behind him, to see the manager about selling his ranch.

Bill Marsden turned at the sound of horses being ridden wildly by a noisy band of cowboys. A cold feeling of dread settled in his stomach. This was what he had been afraid of. Jim Russell stopped ahead of his gang, pulling viciously on his reins, his horse's head coming up, the bit in its mouth biting deep. Leaping down he threw the reins over the hitch rail. Walking into the saloon he checked both guns on his hips. Stepping to one side in the gloom, he let his eyes become accustomed to the light and shadow, before he moved to the bar. The rest of the gang followed in behind him.

'Six beers.' Russell threw the money on the bar as he ordered. 'Who's marshal now?' he demanded of the bartender

'It's me, Russell and when you have finished your drink you can leave town.' Bill Marsden had entered the saloon as Russell had been making his enquiries. Turning from the bar, Russell's hand dropped to his gun.

'Marsden, my old friend.' His piggy eyes weighed up the marshal. 'I thought you were dead long ago.'

Marsden looked the gang over sizing each of them up, trying to see who would prove to be the most dangerous. They were a rough looking lot, all well armed and looking for trouble. Jim Russell let his hand drop from his gun. A fast gun himself he knew of Marsden's reputation. The question was had age slowed him down? Russell was not a man to take chances. The marshal moved forward, looking at Russell.

'I know what you are thinking and there is only one way to find out.' Bill Marsden made his first mistake. He came nearer to Russell, confident of his own reputation. The sound of the heel of a boot hitting the floor made him turn. That was his second and last mistake. Russell was drawing as he turned back. When Russell fired, the bullet hit him on his belt line. His own gun fell from his fingers as he clutched at his stomach to stem the blood which was oozing out. The gun fired again as he fell. A hole appeared between his eyes. His hat left the back of his head with brains, blood and bone-splinters inside of it. The old lawman twitched and lay still.

For a moment nobody moved. Then some left hastily whilst others, unable to move, stared at Bill Marsden's dead body. He had been a good and fair marshal who had kept Silver City a law-abiding town. What would happen now?

Jim Russell's eyes whipped round the room as he shouted, 'You all saw that. He pushed me into it. Jim Russell's my name. Drinks all round and somebody get the undertaker. Marsden's beginning to over-stay his welcome.' Two of his men laughingly pulled the body away from the bar as their drinks were served. The silent animosity of the people who came in to drink and look was beginning to worry him. Calling his men together they went outside.

'It's time to move on but we're short of money. The bank must be bursting with cash. I say we take it.' He checked his guns, replenishing the empty cylinders. The rest followed suit. Russell detailed two of his men to get their horses ready. He stood in the street, looking about, getting his bearings. The bank, on the opposite side further down, caught his attention. A number of horses, tied to the rail, made him hesitate. That meant customers.

'Make your way to the bank then follow me in. Pepe, you come up with the horses.' Arriving at the bank, Russell looked in. A few customers were being attended to. They came out as the gunman entered. He ordered one of his men to stay by the door with instructions not to let anyone in. As he approached the cashier, the office door opened and Flynn came out with Bates and the manager, having completed their transaction.

Jim Russell drew his gun, 'Stay where you

are,' he ordered. The three men stopped in their tracks. John Bates froze clutching the saddle-bag containing the cash payment for his ranch.

'Drop that,' Jim Russell rasped before ordering one of his men to retrieve the fallen saddle-bag. As the gang member crossed Flynn's path he lunged at him. Russell fired, injuring Pat Flynn in the shoulder and knocking him back into the manager's office. He then turned to the cashier. 'Get the money out. Quick. Right, grab the cash you can see and let's go.' His men moved rapidly. John Bates stood behind the counter with the manager. Nobody came in from outside. The gunshot seemed to have gone unnoticed. Russell made for the door. Passing the manager's office, he caught a glimpse of Pat Flynn, struggling to rise. He paused just long enough to pump two more shots into Pat Flynn. The outlaws ran outside, where Pepe was waiting with their horses. It had taken just over five minutes for the robbery.

The milking finished, George Tobias and Mano began to load the milk churns, as Elly came out of the ranch-house ready for the trip into town. 'You go with Mano and I'll put the herd to graze,' Tobias said. He did not want to go to town so soon after the shooting the night before. He had talked it over with Elly and Pat Flynn and had decided to let things settle for a while. Tobias watched them depart before returning to his tasks. Chores completed he went into the bunk-house, took out his Colt and oiled and cleaned it. After checking the shells in his belt, he put it on, holstered the gun and went outside to practise his draw. He took two cans from the garbage heap. Throwing them out in the open he drew his Colt, his hand a blur and fired six shots. Each can was hit three times before it stopped bouncing. The Colt was back in its holster long before the cans came to a halt. He had always found it easy to draw and shoot. Tobias knew no one could beat him and if he had to kill he would do so and not worry too much about it. He unbuckled his gun belt and rolling it up, he put it back in the bunk-house. Then he began his usual fitness training routine. He alternated the skipping with other exercises to improve his stamina and sharpen his reflexes. The actions were automatic and his thoughts wandered to Elly Morgan. He wished Pat was there to talk to. He realized that he was falling in love with Elly and he did not know what to do about it.

Riding into town, Elly Morgan felt more settled than she had done for a long time. Todd Bates and Mark Edge were gone and she no longer had to fear their harassment. Unbelievably, John Bates had decided to sell up and leave the area. Flynn and Tobias were soon to be her neighbours. She realized that her feelings for Tobias were somewhat more than 'neighbourly'.

Mano was holding the reins, letting the horse trot on in its own time. As they approached the outskirts of Silver City, they heard a number of shots being fired. Nearing a bend in the trail, the sound of galloping horses ahead made Mano tug on the reins, pulling the cart to the side of the road. He stopped it as the riders came sweeping round the bend in a cloud of dust.

Russell was in the lead, swearing and cursing at the prospect of more danger. The gang pulled up, horses turning and milling around. Jim Russell drew his gun. Seeing an old Mexican at the reins, he realized that there was no danger. Then he saw Elly Morgan, blonde hair tied back, holding on to the side of the milk cart. In that instance he knew he wanted her. The excitement was still in his blood. The shooting in town, the chase out;

he knew that what he needed now was a woman to top off an exciting day. His instinctive reaction was to reach out for her. Mano cursed him and reached for his whip. That was when Russell hit him with the barrel of his gun, knocking him from the cart to the ground with a vicious blow to the head. Holstering his gun, he grabbed Elly, and threw her across his saddle. Holding the struggling woman, he spurred his horse away.

Five miles out of town, the gang stopped in a copse. The struggling Elly was thrown screaming to the ground. Jim Russell jumped down from his horse. Standing over a dazed Elly Morgan, he turned to his men.

'Keep watch. Your turn will come when I've finished with her.' Reaching down he pulled at her shirt top, ripping it open he gripped her breast. Elly Morgan kicked up at him, catching his thigh with her boot.

'Keep still, you bitch.' He back-handed her to the side of her face, knocking her unconscious. He took his gun belt off, dropping it to the ground and reaching down he pulled up her riding skirt and tore away at her under-garments. Her bared body raised a lust in him. Elly Morgan moaned as he thrust himself into her. His hands squeezed her breasts, the pain bringing Elly back to her senses. Horror etched on her face as she realized what was happening. The hardness of Russell hurt her as his grunting tempo increased. She tried to pull away as he released himself but he had her pinned helplessly to the ground. Her struggles and screams roused him again. This time his invasion went on longer.

Elly closed her eyes trying to wipe out of her mind what was happening to her. He shuddered again as he finished. She lay still as he withdrew himself. Perhaps now they would leave her alone. She heard Russell call for Pepe. She shuddered as she felt a hand on her. Then again the weight of a body on hers. She knew then that all of them were going to take her. After the third member of the gang had defiled her, she wanted to die of shame.

'Tobias. Where are you?' she screamed, before passing out, again.

'Who is this Tobias?' asked Pepe, as he stood watching another of the gang abuse her.

'Who cares,' Jim Russell answered as he counted the money that they had stolen from the bank, 'This is bonanza-time boys. There's thousands here.' The knowledge only increased and intensified their 'pleasure' of Elly

Morgan. Hours later the gang was on its way, leaving the bruised and bleeding woman lying unconscious and uncovered in the copse.

Tobias began to worry. He had expected Elly and Mano back before now. He saddled one of the horses and headed towards town, hoping to meet them returning home, possibly accompanied by Pat Flynn with the deeds for John Bates's ranch. His thoughts jerked back to the present when he spotted the stationary cart. Within seconds Tobias was alongside it. The horse was grazing at the side of the trail and Mano was slumped alongside the cart, the reins still in his hand. There was no sign of Elly Morgan. He stooped and effortlessly picked up Mano and set him on the wagon-seat. Getting his water bottle he poured some on a cloth and wiped Mano's injured forehead before trying to pour some water down his throat. Mano came to with a splutter and Tobias helped him take a drink.

'Mano,' Tobias spoke softly to the old Mexican. 'Mano, where's Miss Elly? What happened here?'

Mano tried to speak. 'Many men came from town, shooting.' He raised his hand to his head, as if trying to clear it. 'Miss Elly?

59

They must have took her.'

Supporting Mano on the cart, with his horse trailing behind, Tobias headed for Silver City. Crowds of people were still outside the bank when he arrived. He drove past to Doctor Burgess's surgery. Stopping the wagon, he picked up Mano and carried him into the building, as Bill Campbell came out with the mayor of Silver City.

'Tobias, I'm glad to see you,' Campbell said. On his chest was the marshal's badge. Tobias did not stop to talk. He entered the surgery with the mayor and Campbell at his heels.

The doctor was washing his hands. He came over, showing concern. 'Not another shooting?' he said.

Tobias put Mano down. 'No,' he answered. 'He's had a nasty blow to the head. What's happening out there?' Campbell told him of the mayhem caused by Jim Russell's gang – the killing of Marsden, the bank hold-up and the shooting down of Pat Flynn.

'Where's Pat now?' Tobias asked.

The doctor turned from Mano. 'He's resting in the back. He'll be OK.'

'Tobias, Miss Elly.' Mano spoke, as his senses fully returned. 'They must have took her and rode away.' At the sound of the

Mexican's voice Tobias came back to him.

'Who took her Mano? Who?' Mano's head was clearing now. He told them about hearing shots and the gang coming out of town in such a hurry.

'That settles it,' said Campbell. 'It's Russell's gang. We'll get a posse together and go after them.'

'But it's chaos since the marshal was killed,' the mayor butted in. 'There's no one to organize a posse. They'll be miles away by now.'

'Are you afraid of them?' Tobias's voice was low and angry. 'They have Miss Elly.' He turned to Mano. 'Which way did they go, Mano?' The old Mexican shook his head sadly.

'Russell has a broken-down spread out Tombstone way. He could be heading there,' Bill Campbell offered.

Mano got shakily to his feet. 'I will go with you, Tobias.'

'I'll have a look at Pat and then I will go after them myself,' he glowered. He entered the back room to find Flynn sleeping, swathed in bandages. The doctor joined him. 'Will he recover, Doctor?' The concern showed in Tobias's voice.

'He should be OK but he must have rest

now.' He guided Tobias out of the room and shut the door.

'I would go with you but I am needed here,' said Campbell. 'The townsfolk are a bit restless with the bank losing money and all. We don't know how they will react.' Tobias saw the sense in his reasoning.

'I will go after them but not for the money. If Miss Elly's been harmed by them...' His anger swelled up, cutting off his words. 'Mano. Let's go home.' The old Mexican followed the giant Negro out. Not much was said on the way back to the ranch. Mano was still shaken. Tobias was busy making plans for his revenge on Jim Russell's gang. He left Mano to cook a meal whilst he collected the things he would need – rifle, ammunition, blankets, food and water. Mano called him interrupting his thoughts. His meal was ready. The food was simple and nourishing. Tobias ate heartily – eating more than his fill – as he did not want to be stopped by hunger in his search for Elly and the gang.

Leaving a protesting Mano behind to look after the ranch, he returned to where he had found the stationary milk cart. He picked up the trail where a number of horses had stopped and then moved away. Tobias followed, hoping he was on the right track.

One set of hoof-prints was deeper than the rest which told Tobias that one horse was carrying two people. As dusk fell, Tobias began to worry. He had travelled at a steady pace but had wasted a lot of time dismounting, checking, walking. Finally his tracking brought him to the copse. Dismounting, he entered the trees. Stepping silently and carefully he came across the still, prone, naked body of Elly Morgan. He stopped in his tracks. She was dead. The crumpled, motionless figure could not be alive. He was at her side, touching her, raising her by her shoulders. She moaned. He gently lowered her back to the ground. Grabbing a bundle from his horse he was back at her side. The blanket was wrapped round the naked, inert form that was Elly. He bathed her bruised face and moistened her swollen lips from his water bottle. Tears blurred his vision as he spoke her name. Thoughts of going after Jim Russell temporarily forgotten, he spoke gently to Elly as he continued to bathe her face.

Her eyes opened. 'Tobias,' she said. He soothed her bruised face and gave her more water. She gagged, turning her face away. Then she began to recall what had happened to her, the pains in her body bringing back the horrors of her ordeal. She screamed, cowering away from Tobias, her sobs reaching down into his soul. The giant Negro picked up the sobbing Elly in his arms, her body shaking violently and walked with her to where his horse was tethered. Cradling her in his left arm, he made his way back to Silver City. Arriving there in the early hours of the morning, he headed for Doc Burgess's surgery. His frenzied knocking brought the doctor to the door. On seeing Tobias cradling Elly he ushered them in calling for his wife to come and help.

'You rest while I examine her,' said the doctor. The doctor's wife gave him some coffee and left him waiting in the parlour. He fell asleep in the armchair and was later roused by the doctor. Jumping to his feet he asked how Miss Elly was. The doctor sat down. Exhaustion set on his face. It had been a busy twenty-four hours, what with the shootings and Elly Morgan's assault. The lack of sleep was taking its toll.

'She's in a bad way. Outside the bruising isn't too bad but internally...' The doctor shook his head before continuing, 'She's been very badly abused. There is internal damage. Mrs Burgess is looking after her.'

'Can I see her?' Tobias asked.

64

'Only for a short time,' the doctor answered.

Tobias entered the room and stood by the bed. The bruised, swollen face of Elly was all he could see. Her eyes were closed. Her breathing broken by sobs. Vengeance was all he could feel for Jim Russell and his gang of cut-throats. They had nearly destroyed the two people he held most dear. Tobias left the room.

'Can I see Pat now?'

The doctor led him into the room where Pat Flynn lay with his eyes wide open. 'What are you looking so unhappy about Tobias? I'm not that bad, am I, Doc?' It was evident that Pat Flynn was going to make a good recovery. Tobias took his hand, as the doctor checked the dressings and wounds – nodding his head at what he saw – obviously very pleased at the progress and improvement in his patient.

'I'll leave you to talk while I rustle up some breakfast.' The doctor shut the door behind him as he left. The big Negro told Pat Flynn what had happened since Jim Russell and his gang had hit Silver City. Flynn took the news, of the attack on Elly Morgan, badly.

'I'm going after them, Pat. I will find them if it takes me the rest of my life.' Flynn had never seen Tobias show so much hatred, not even when they had found Philip Tobias after the raid.

'Wait till I get back on my feet and we will go together,' Flynn offered.

Tobias shook his head. 'I can't wait that long, Pat. They could be anywhere by then.'

Flynn knew it was a waste of time arguing with him. 'Watch your step then, me boyo. Don't let your anger get you killed.'

Tobias left the doctor's house and headed for the ranch to tell Mano what had happened and what he was going to do. After his talk with Mano he returned to the copse where he had found Elly Morgan. He began looking for any sign left by Russell and his gang. The signs, where the attack had taken place, were there to be seen. The flattened grass, encircled by cigarette-ends and footprints, where they had stood watching each other. Following the signs, where they had left the copse, he mounted and set off. He knew he would find them and when he did...

He clenched his fist in anger.

# FOUR

Darkness found him sitting by his fire, his second cup of coffee in his hand. What would they be doing now? he wondered. His anger was now under control. He brooded on Russell. What kind of an animal was he to shoot Pat when he was lying wounded on the floor and then beat a defenceless old man like Mano? And Elly? The coffee tasted bitter as the thoughts ran through his mind. Tossing the dregs into the fire he turned in for the night.

First sign of dawn saw him rekindling the fire. Using some of the food Mano had packed, he cooked a meal large enough to last him all day, before setting off again. He picked up the gang's trail, which headed west. Bill Campbell had said that Russell had a spread around Tombstone and it looked as if he was heading that way. Feeling more confident, Tobias increased his horse's gait. He made good progress in the light of day. Finding a good camping-site for the night, his thoughts turned to Elly Morgan and Pat Flynn. Tomorrow would be his third day. He knew Pat would be on the mend but what about Elly? The doctor had been concerned for both her physical and mental state.

He closed his eyes. The sounds of the night came to him. Animals calling to each other. He lay listening. Sleep did not come quickly. Again his thoughts turned to vengeance, to Russell and how he would kill him. A new sound caught his attention. This time it was different. It broke into his thoughts. Tobias rose silently, moving away from the dying fire, his gun in his hand. Crouching low, he waited. Whoever it was moved slowly. He could hear the shuffling. He saw a figure stagger and fall, rise and fall again. Tobias heard a cry as the shape tried unsuccessfully to rise. Moving in its direction, not making a sound, his gun to hand, Tobias approached cautiously. On reaching the prone figure, he leant over, touching it. He was surprised to find it was an Indian squaw. At his touch she pulled away. Her hair was dishevelled, covering her face, and her clothes were ripped and torn. Defiantly, she kicked out at Tobias.

He holstered his gun and stood back. 'I'm not going to hurt you.' The squaw lay still, not fully understanding the way Tobias spoke. Leaving her, Tobias went back to his camp. Stirring the dying coals of his fire, he poured some coffee into a cup and took it back to her. She drank the warm liquid, gulping some of it and spitting the rest out. She stared at Tobias, not sure if she could trust him. He offered his hand. 'I won't harm you,' he said gently.

She let him help her to her feet. Tobias led her to his camp-fire and motioned for her to sit down. Taking the blanket he offered, she pulled it closely around her scantily clothed body. Tobias turned away. Pouring some water into a bowl, he gave her a towel and left her to clean herself in private. He was anxious to know what had happened to her. She had obviously been involved in some kind of a skirmish. Where were the rest of her companions? Had she been alone? He turned his attention back to her. Her brown eyes, glittering in the firelight, stared at Tobias.

'White men come. Take Nahita. Do this thing.' She opened the blanket to show her body. The vision of Elly came to him as she spoke.

'How many?' Tobias moved closer. The squaw cowered away, clutching the blanket. Tobias stood back. 'No. How many?' he repeated, putting up his hand. 'White men.

How many? One? Two?' He counted on his fingers.

The squaw, realizing what he meant, took a twig from the edge of the fire and marked six times on the ground. Tobias felt the excitement. They could not be far ahead. It looked as if they had attacked the squaw while she was away from her canip. Something must have disturbed them. Fear of retribution from her village braves probably accounted for them leaving her still alive.

The shadows appeared in the firelight before Tobias knew they were there. Tobias froze. They were surrounded by Indians. He kept his hand away from his gun. The squaw stood up, speaking in her native tongue. The leader of the braves answered back and the squaw pointed away, in the direction she had come from. More questions. A show of anger. They centred their attention on Tobias.

'They say, why you here?'

Tobias told her briefly. She translated his words to the leader. Taking out his knife, he came and stood in front of Tobias, whose hand dropped to his gun. 'No. Take.' He passed the knife to Tobias, handle first. Tobias took it. The leader spoke to the squaw and the group left as quietly as they had arrived. The squaw sat down by the fire, the blanket around her, staring into the flames. The quietness of the night set in. Tobias stood, the Indian's knife still in his hand. 'Why didn't you go with them?' he asked.

'No. I stay. Go with you.' She came and stood in front of him, taking the knife from him. 'I find white men. You shoot.' She reverted to her own native tongue as she grabbed his groin, slashing with the knife. 'I finish them.' The knife was handed back to Tobias.

She thinks she's coming with me, thought Tobias. She and the braves must have agreed on it. Tobias pulled his blanket round him. 'We will see what tomorrow brings.'

The hand shook him gently. 'Eat, then we go.' Tobias came awake wondering, then he recalled the events of the previous evening. He felt in his boot. The knife was still there. The squaw was watching his every move. She had fixed her clothing, making herself more presentable. She was younger than he thought. Pretty, in a fashion. The black hair swept back, he could see the bruises on her face. She turned away ashamed under his scrutiny.

'You must go back to your home. You can't come with me. You will be in the way.'

She stared at Tobias. 'I have no home. Not till white men dead.' She stood watching as Tobias saddled and mounted his horse. He patted the horse's rump, signalling her to climb up behind him. Nahita shook her head and set off ahead of Tobias, following the trail. Her shuffling gait only slowed when the signs petered out. Then she searched, moving grass and rocks, before moving on again. When night came they made camp and ate in silence. It was colder than the previous night. They lay either side of the fire. During the night he felt the slight figure of the squaw climb in under his blanket. The other blanket was wrapped round them and he went back to sleep, much warmer.

The next morning saw them up before dawn and on the trail. Tobias's offer to ride was again turned down by Nahita. Later in the day the town of Tombstone came into view. Nahita slowed and pointed. 'Here,' she said.

They made camp outside of town and made plans. The squaw slipped into Tombstone on her own. She returned to tell Tobias that two of her attackers were in town. There was no sign of the rest of them. Tobias checked his gun and drew it a few times. Pulling the knife from his boot, he gave it to

Nahita. It disappeared immediately inside her clothing. She led the way back into town.

Tombstone was a bustling community. Mingling with the crowd they stopped outside the saloon. Nahita peered through the window. A Mexican left a table, bought two drinks and returned, giving one to his partner. Both were pointed out to Tobias.

After asking for directions to the Russell spread, Tobias left town, with the squaw trotting alongside him. They turned on to the trail leading towards Jim Russell's ranch and there they waited patiently for the two members of his gang to return home.

The first the two outlaws knew of any danger was when the two shapes appeared out of the darkness, in front of them. The little Mexican slowed, swaying drunkenly in his saddle. 'What do you want?' he asked, peering into the darkness, as the big rider came towards him. 'Who are you?' His speech was slurred. The big rider stopped. The slight figure alongside pressed closer to the horse.

'My name's Tobias,' he said. His hand came up. His gun fired two shots. Both men fell from their horses. The mounts, shying away, stopped. The slight figure of the squaw shuffled forward, her hand going into her clothing. With the knife flashing in her hand, she knelt by the Mexican. Her hand gripped his groin. His eyes stared in terror as the knife bit deep. The pain from the bullet wound was forgotten. He saw the squaw's face staring. She spat at him as she pulled and cut. The spittle ran down his face. The terrible scream did not move Tobias. As he watched Nahita, his thoughts were of Elly Morgan and how she must have felt on that terrible night. The squaw moved to the other outlaw. He was dead. The bullet had hit him in the heart. In silence, Nahita completed her task. Having accomplished part of their mission they returned to their camp, outside of Tombstone.

Tobias stayed in camp next day. Nahita, wrapped in a blanket, shuffled round town listening to talk. The two murders were the main topic of conversation. At first it was thought to be robbery but money was found on the bodies. A grudge killing was then thought to be the cause.

Nahita saw Jim Russell with a member of his gang. She watched as they came out of the saloon and made their way to the local whorehouse. At this point, Nahita left town. Tobias spotted her coming his way. He mounted his horse and went to meet her, on the trail. On hearing that Jim Russell was in town, he pulled her up behind him. She pointed out the whorehouse as they made their way to the stables. The outlaws' horses were still there. The owner came out and took Tobias's horse. 'Give him a good rub. I will be back soon.'

'That will be a dollar.' The stable owner took the money and stood watching the strange couple as they went off.

They made their way to the brothel. Tobias entered first, Nahita squeezing in behind him. A woman approached him.

'Well, well. Another early bird. Most of the girls are sleeping off a heavy night.' Then she noticed the squaw. 'You can't bring your own whores here.' She laughed at her own coarse joke.

'I'm looking for Jim Russell,' Tobias said. 'I'm to meet him here.'

'He's up in room two. Scott Benson's in room four,' she said, nodding towards the stairs.

Tobias and Nahita climbed the stairs. Passing number two, Tobias paused and listened. He could hear a couple talking. He carried on to number four. He tried the door and it opened to his touch. Stepping quickly inside, the squaw close on his heels, his gun came out.

The man called Scott Benson turned from his position between the whore's legs. 'What do you want?' Anger and then surprise appeared on his face, at the sight of the giant Negro holding the gun.

'Stay where you are.' The woman opened her mouth to scream. 'Don't make a sound. It doesn't concern you.' Tobias moved nearer to the naked couple. He placed his gun behind Benson's ear. 'Is he one of them?' he asked Nahita. She nodded. 'Well, what are you waiting for?' said Tobias. Benson watched over his shoulder as the squaw approached the foot of the bed. He saw her take the knife from the folds of her clothing.

'What do you want? I don't know you,' he said with fear creeping into his voice, as he withdrew from the whore. Tobias's gun pushed harder into his ear and Nahita took hold of his manhood. The knife came up, slashing through his soft flesh. It was done before Benson realized what was happening. The whore lay mesmerized with fear. Tobias's gun crashed down on Benson's head, putting him out of his pain and misery. Tobias holstered his gun and left the room, moving on to number two. He paused for a second before opening the door and drawing his gun he went in. Jim Russell was dressing, his back to the door. The whore had left. There was nobody else in the room.

'Jim Russell?' Tobias spoke. Russell turned to face him. Surprised to see the giant Negro standing before him, his hand dropped to his gun. 'Don't.' The command stopped him. 'I will give you a chance. That's more than you gave the people you shot in Silver City.'

Jim Russell smirked. 'And they've sent you to get me?' There was confidence now in his voice. 'I'm not alone. If you shoot me, Benson will get you.' Nahita came into the room, the knife gripped in her hand, blood still on the blade.

'Benson won't be any good to anybody,' said Tobias, 'especially women. He's lost all his desire, the same as your Mexican friend, last night.'

Realizing that he was facing the killer of his two men, Russell took a closer look at the squaw. It slowly dawned on him who she was. 'Who are you?' he asked the Negro.

'George Tobias,' came the answer.

'Tobias. The girl from Silver City mentioned you,' Russell taunted him, hoping to distract him. 'She was nice. Very nice.'

Tobias holstered his gun. 'You won't do it again,' he said. Russell stared at him, undecided. Tobias stood – no sign of nerves – waiting. As Russell's arm dropped down to his gun, the bullet hit him in the stomach, knocking him back against the bed. His gun fell to the floor. Russell could not believe he had been shot. The pain was agonizing. Then the Indian squaw came to him. Her hand gripped his groin. The knife cut his pants as he pulled away. The grip tightened as the blade sliced. She spat in his face. His screams echoed around the whorehouse. People passing stopped and listened and stared as the black man and the Indian squaw came out and walked in the direction of the stables. Tobias rode away from Tombstone with Nahita mounted behind him.

Once they were clear of the town, Tobias slowed his mount and, turning in on to the trail leading to the Russell spread, he trotted his horse till he came in sight of the dilapidated buildings. Neglect was everywhere. Tobias stopped his horse to let Nahita slide off the back. He then approached the front of the house. Boards had replaced glass at some of the windows. The door opened. A face appeared, stubbled and dirty.

'What do you want?' A rifle came into view.

'Is this Jim Russell's place?' asked Tobias.

The unkempt figure opened the door and stepped outside at the mention of Jim Russell's name. The rifle was still pointing at Tobias. A noise from one of the windows and a gun-barrel appearing convinced Tobias that his quest for revenge was nearing its end. What he had to do now was to get the two men together.

'I met Russell in town with a man called Benson. He said he had a spread and told me he might be able to use me. It seems he's short-handed as two of his men met with some kind of accident, last night.'

'Duke,' the man with the rifle shouted back into the house. The gun-barrel vanished from the window, to appear with its owner at the door. 'Did you hear what he said?'

'I heard,' Duke growled, weighing up the Negro. Then he looked at the squaw, wrapped up in the blanket. 'Is she yours or do you share it?'

Tobias shrugged his wide shoulders. 'She does what I say.'

'Come in. Let's have a drink.' Duke seemed to be in charge.

The inside of the house was as derelict as the outside. Looking for somewhere to sit Tobias found a chair, away from the gang members. Nahita stood behind him, her head lowered, the blanket pulled tight around her.

Duke put his rifle down. 'What did Jim say then?'

'When we left him, he was screaming,' said Tobias, drawing his gun, and shooting Duke's partner, who still held his rifle. The rifle fell to the floor as the bullet hit him in the shoulder. Duke reached for his gun as Tobias's second shot hit him in the knee, shattering it. Both men lay groaning on the floor with Tobias standing over them.

'A lot of money was taken from the bank in Silver City. I want to know where it is,' he said. Both men remained silent. 'I'll ask you one more time.'

'We haven't been to Silver City,' Duke moaned.

'I've followed you from there. Jim Russell is dead along with Benson.' Tobias pointed his gun at Duke.

'Go to hell,' Duke snarled. Tobias's gun exploded. The bullet shattered his other knee. Tobias turned to Duke's partner, who was clutching his shoulder.

'Where's the money?' he asked.

The groaning Duke hissed, 'Don't tell him.'

Nahita moved at Tobias's command and crouched over the blood stained outlaw. The knife cut deep. The blood gushed from his groin to meet the blood from his shattered knees. She spat at the writhing Duke, then she turned to the other wounded outlaw.

'Don't let her touch me. I'll tell you where the money is,' he whined, in terror. 'It's in the bedroom, inside one of the pillows.'

Tobias's search was fruitful. He took the pillow with the money inside.

A shout of 'No. Please don't,' had Tobias hurrying back into the room, to see the knife coming away and the squaw spitting on the last member of the Russell gang. Leaving the two men, in their death throes, writhing on the floor, Tobias and Nahita left the house. Mounting his horse Tobias rode away with Nahita up behind him. He dug in his heels and headed his mount in the direction of Silver City.

## FIVE

That night, well away from the Jim Russell spread, Tobias made camp for himself and the Indian squaw. Lying in his blanket he went over the events of the last few days.

Between them they had wiped out the whole Jim Russell gang. Nobody would know who he was or why he had come after them. He turned to look at the bundle at the other side of the camp-fire. He had shared her company now for three or four days and yet he knew nothing about her other than their mutual quest for revenge. She had used the knife on the six white men without hesitation. Only now did he realize that her cool determination had resulted in the speedy execution of their revenge.

As if sensing his scrutiny, she turned and looked across at Tobias, the fire reflected in her eyes. Tobias felt an urge in his loins. A desire which he had felt before, when he had been close to Elly Morgan. He had kept it under control then and did so now. The giant Negro closed his eyes. His blanket moved and the brown, naked body of the Indian girl was lying next to him. It was the first time that he had experienced the intimate touch of a woman. Nahita's hand touched and stroked him. His arousal was instant. She came closer. The softness of her thighs enveloped him. He lay still as the soft body moved and groaned. Tobias could feel his discharge building up inside of him. Then it was flowing out as Nahita met him, her thighs squeezing him. A shiver ran through her body. Then she was gone, as silently as she had arrived. Contentment spread through his body and sleep soon enveloped him.

The aroma of cooking awoke him. He studied the silent figure busy at the fire. Nahita lowered her eyes as she offered him the food. Not a word was spoken between them. It was as if last night had never happened. That day she ran alongside his mount. She had declined to ride behind him.

Later on that day a group of Indian braves approached them. Tobias stopped. Loosening his gun, he waited. Nahita, showing signs of excitement, left his side to go and meet them. Tobias watched them converse. Their leader, the brave who had given him the knife, rode to meet him, with Nahita trotting alongside. This time he spoke in English and not through Nahita. He had come to thank Tobias for helping to restore his daughter's honour after the rape by the white men. He was Chief Big Eagle, of the Sioux, and he would be proud if the big black warrior would take the knife she had used to avenge her shame. He handed the knife over.

'If you have trouble, Chief Big Eagle help you.' Then he spoke in his own tongue to Nahita, who in turn thanked Tobias. The

Indian chief reached down from his horse and took a rawhide bag from his daughter. Opening it, he tossed the contents to the wind. Bloodstained testicles flew about in all directions. With a cry he pulled Nahita up behind him and rode away to join his party and vanish in the distance.

Tobias pushed his horse along at a steady gait now. He wanted to get back to Silver City as soon as possible. It was a tired Tobias who unsaddled his horse in the stables and paid the night attendant two dollars to rub and feed his mount. Silver City seemed busier than usual. The saloons were noisy. Drunken miners and cowboys pushed their way from place to place. The big Negro avoided them, not wanting to get involved in any trouble.

Tobias walked to the doctor's house, where a light could be seen in the surgery. He was glad that the doctor was still up. Somewhere a window was broken and gunshots could be heard. The marshal was in for a busy night, he thought as he knocked on the door. A call of 'Who's there,' surprised Tobias.

'George Tobias,' he answered. He heard bolts being drawn. A nervous doctor looked out. A look of relief spread across the doctor's face at the sight of him.

'Come in, quick.' The door was shut and bolted behind him.

'What's wrong, Doctor? How's Miss Elly and Pat?'

'They're all right. Both improving. It's Campbell.' He peered through the curtains nervously. 'In here.' He guided Tobias into a bedroom, where Bill Campbell was lying on a bed with his head and body swathed in bandages. A pale Pat Flynn was standing over him.

'Tobias.' The pleased Irishman came round to grip his friend's hand, 'Am I glad to see you, son.'

'What's going on, Pat?' Tobias asked after the pleasantries were over.

'There's a gambler, called Lew Jenks, who came into town a few days ago. He shot and killed a miner the first night he was here. The miner had accused him of cheating and Jenks drew and shot him. He has a partner with him. A Jim Buckley, who's a fast gun, though they say Jenks doesn't need him. He could be a card-shark – I don't know – but he seldom loses. Campbell enquired about the shooting and ordered him out of town. Jenks pistol-whipped him then Buckley shot him in the back as he lay on the floor.

Campbell's been lying here now for two days. The doc said he may not pull through. Jenks said that if he does he'll shoot him again. That's why the door is locked.'

Tobias sat down, exhausted. 'If Miss Elly is able to travel, I will take her out of here, back to the ranch. This killing is getting me down. I've just killed six men, Pat, and I've watched an Indian squaw castrate them and I enjoyed it. That can't be right. I need to get away from it all.'

Pat Flynn put his arm around the young giant. He was still only a young man yet everyone was looking to him to save them. 'OK, Tobias, I will go with you in the morning.'

The next morning Tobias returned the stolen money he had retrieved from the Russell gang to the bank. Both he and Flynn tried to persuade Miss Elly to leave the doctor's home and return to her own ranch but she would not move. She was still in a state of shock and fear. The mayor was trying to hire a town marshal. The names of Wyatt Earp and other famous gun-fighters were being mentioned. Now that there was no active marshal, Silver City was becoming an open town. It would not be long before more bad elements arrived to cause more trouble. Flynn and Tobias left town. The two friends were quiet riding to Elly Morgan's spread. They had a lot to think about. Then there was their own ranch, being looked after by the remnants of John Bates's crew who had opted to stay and work for them.

Mano was pleased to see them. After catching up on their chores the duo went to look round their newly acquired ranch. It was a big spread with a good herd of cattle and excellent grazing land. Hank Jay, who had been the ramrod was again left in charge, with orders to contact Flynn or Tobias if any problems arose. On the way back to Miss Elly's ranch, Tobias told Flynn, in more detail, about his encounter with Nahita and the Indian braves, and her part in the killings. He took the knife from his boot and handed it to the Irishman.

'He must have rated you highly to have given you that,' commented Flynn as he handed the knife back to his friend.

Mano had milked the herd while they were away. When they returned, the churns were ready to be loaded on to the milk cart, to go into town. While Pat Flynn rested, Tobias took the milk into Silver City. He called at the doctor's to see Miss Elly and Bill Campbell. The old buffalo hunter was making slow progress. Elly Morgan still would not leave the doctor's wife's side. Boarding the cart, he headed back to the ranch. He still had not seen Jenks or his gunman Buckley and that pleased him, for he did not want any dealings with either of them. Riding out of town he passed groups of cowboys riding in. New faces – all toting guns tied down on their thighs. He told Pat what he had seen. It did not please him. It looked as if the word had spread about Silver City being an open town with no lawman. The scum of the badlands were coming in to make a killing.

After a few days with Pat Flynn, Tobias became more relaxed. Flynn was getting stronger every day. The ranch they had bought was doing well. Hank Jay was proving to be a good ramrod. That morning the two friends decided to take the milk load into town. Pat Flynn jumped aboard the cart, placing his rifle at his feet. Tobias climbed up alongside of him, his pistol in its holster, rolled up and placed beside Flynn's rifle.

'If I don't wear it, I won't have to use it,' said Tobias. Flynn nodded in agreement. Nearing town they came up behind two riders. Both rode in the centre of the trail, neither giving way. Pat pulled on the reins, slowing behind the two men, who refused to pull over to the side to let the cart through. As they entered the town, they eased over, to let them pass. Not wanting to cause trouble Pat ignored the two riders. As they drew level, one of them drew his gun and fired it under the body of the carthorse. The animal bolted, scattering people in its wake. Pat Flynn fought to get it under control as two milk churns bounced off the cart, spilling their contents. His expert handling brought the horse under control. Turning the horse in a circle, he stopped it alongside the two riders, who were dismounting outside the saloon. Both men were laughing as Flynn and Tobias approached.

'You two fools could have got somebody killed.' It was Flynn who spoke as he neared them. One of the two dropped his hand to his gun.

'If you don't want killing, old man, go peddle your milk.'

Flynn climbed down and hit him, knocking him to the ground. As he clawed for his gun, Flynn kicked it from his hand, then reached down and pulled him to his feet. Hitting him again, he floored him once more. This time he did not move. The other cow-hand pulled his gun as Pat Flynn turned to face him. Tobias stepped between them. His left hand stopped the gun from levelling and shooting the Irishman. His right hand, with the Indian knife in it, plunged up to the hilt into the cow-hand's stomach. Tobias pulled the knife out. The gun fired into the ground and then fell from the lifeless fingers. The body crumpled to the ground. Pat Flynn gripped Tobias and pulled him away as a crowd began to gather.

Lew Jenks was eating a late breakfast when the commotion outside interrupted him. Groups of people, hurrying past the window, aroused his interest. 'Go see what's causing the commotion,' he told Jim Buckley.

Buckley followed the hurrying crowd. He was just in time to see Tobias sink his knife into the stomach of the rider. Then he saw Pat Flynn pull him away and lead him to the cart. The look of hatred on the Negro's face made his innards go cold. A shudder ran through him. He had never seen hatred, etched so raw, before. He himself had faced the emotion often enough, but what he had just seen, on the big man's face, was something he hoped he would never have to confront himself. He knew that if that rider had got up from the ground, the black giant would have cut him to pieces. The dead man's saddle-mate rose. He staggered to where his partner lay in a crumpled heap. The sight of blood and his open stomach made him retch.

'Who did this?' he shouted, kneeling beside the body.

Jim Buckley approached him. 'I know who killed him. You tend to your friend and I'll see you in the Main Chance saloon later. The name's Jim Buckley.'

'Lee Grant's my name and this is my brother Don.'

Jim Buckley put a hand on his shoulder and gave him a few comforting words, before reporting the events to Lew Jenks. After listening to Buckley's account with interest, he decided to accompany him and meet Grant.

'We might be able to use this young hot-head. The Negro may be the one called Tobias. The fast gun everyone talks about. We might get to see how fast he is.'

Lee Grant buried his brother and then swore revenge on the man who had killed him. He was the kind of hot-head who caused trouble and then blamed everybody else when things went wrong. Entering the Main Chance saloon he saw Buckley playing cards with Jenks. Both men noted his arrival with interest. They saw his gun was tied down on his right thigh. He was a young man looking for trouble. Buckley called him over and introduced him to Lew Jenks.

'I believe your brother was murdered on your arrival in town today.' The gambler played on his feelings. 'The man that killed him is said to be pretty fast with a gun. If I were you I'd give him a wide berth.'

Jenks could see the recklessness in the young cowboy. 'Are you any good with that?' he asked pointing to Grant's gun.

'I'm good enough for him.' He drew his gun to impress the gambler. It was fast and smooth.

Jenks feigned surprise. 'Very good,' he said. Jenks knew that he was looking at a dead man. A lot of cowboys were fast on the draw and they got the idea in their heads that they could out-draw anybody, but a shooter could be beaten and still kill you. Lew Jenks knew this from past experience. It was keeping a cool nerve that mattered, when facing a man down.

'You might find your brother's killer at the doctor's place. He and his partner usually call on their milk round to see how the marshal is progressing. One's an Irishman, the other a Negro. He's the man with the fast gun. They call him Tobias.'

Lee Grant listened to the sympathy and praise. He knew he was fast and that he could hit his target with accuracy. He and his brother used to practise with cans and bottles. He was always the best shot. They had never faced anybody in a real shoot-out but they were confident that they could and so they had set out to seek fame and fortune, however notorious. Now his brother was dead and he was filled with revenge. In Silver City, a boom town, he had his chance to make his name as a fast gun in pursuit of his brother's killer.

Lew Jenks paid for the drinks as he and Buckley fuelled Lee Grant's desire for vengeance. 'Have a look and see if our *friends* are over at the doctor's yet, Jim.' Buckley obeyed and walked to the saloon doors. The milk cart was tethered outside the surgery.

'It looks like your brother's killer is over at the doctor's,' Jenks remarked, putting the emphasis on the word killer, to stir up the young cowboy's anger. Lee Grant jumped up, a nervousness in his movements. Jenks let him go, watching him hesitate by the door before leaving. Buckley pointed to the milk cart outside the surgery, as he went through the swing doors. Jenks joined Buckley at the window and both watched with interest.

In the doctor's parlour, Tobias sat talking to Miss Elly, while Flynn was in the bedroom talking to Bill Campbell. The marshal had regained his faculties and although he was still confined to the doctor's care he was greatly concerned about the lawless element that was coming in weekly, and of the increase in attacks on miners, bringing in their silver. The miners were talking of taking the law into their own hands. The hope of bringing in a top lawman, such as Earp or Hickok had not matured. Campbell asked Flynn if he and Tobias would be interested. Flynn replied that he felt Tobias had been too much involved in killings, lately. He then told Campbell about the Russell gang and how Tobias had wiped them out and of the Indian involvement. A gun-shot outside interrupted their talk, sending Flynn to the window. Lee Grant was outside, gun in hand, shouting.

Flynn took his rifle and went to the door. Opening it, he stepped outside. He closed the door behind him, not wanting Tobias to get involved if he could help it. Lee Grant faced him as he came out. 'I want the man who killed my brother,' he said. His gun was still in his hand. Flynn watched him. He could see that Grant was uncertain.

'Your brother was killed by a man who didn't carry a gun. Your brother would have shot me if he had not been stopped.' Flynn's rifle pointed unwaveringly at Grant. 'Go home, son. There is nothing to be proved coming here,' said Flynn. 'It was you who started all this.'

Grant's hand shook. He could see Flynn's eyes, unblinking. The Irishman did not say any more. He had given the young cowboy food for thought. They had come into town and caused a ruckus and it had cost his brother his life. The gun was put away as the young cowboy turned and went to his horse, mounted it and left town without looking back. A long sigh of relief escaped from Flynn's lips as he re-entered the doctor's home.

Bill Campbell was the first to speak. 'I think that young man was set up. How did he know that you were here? Ah. There's the answer,' he added as he spotted the gambler and his henchman through the window. 'That's Jenks and Buckley.' Pat Flynn took notice of the men and watched them as they went back into the saloon.

Tobias and Flynn came out of the doctor's

surgery. A shout stopped them climbing aboard the milk cart. A number of miners were coming their way. Flynn raised his rifle; Tobias's gun was lifted from its holster. The largest of them turned out to be Wallace, the miner who had entered the boxing contest and done so well against Joe Burke. It looked as if he was their spokesman.

'Would you and your friend, the rifleman, take the marshal's job, till the mayor gets a top gunfighter to keep law and order?' he asked Tobias. He went on to explain how the miners were being robbed, beaten-up and even murdered by the riff-raff and gunmen who had moved in since the killing of Marshal Bill Marsden. Tobias remained silent. Pat Flynn told them that they had had enough of shooting.

'Why don't you get some guns and defend yourselves?' Pat asked him.

'We can fight but we are not gunslingers,' Wallace pleaded.

Tobias spoke up before Pat Flynn could answer. 'Very well. I will take the job.'

Wallace gripped his hand, thanking him. 'Come on. We will drink to that.' The miners pulled Tobias and Pat Flynn towards the Main Chance saloon. Wallace pushed open the doors. 'We've got ourselves a marshal,' he shouted, leading the way to the bar, ordering drinks all round. 'You want to shut down some of these poker games and make sure the rest are straight.' Wallace made his comments as he looked over to Jenks's table.

The gambler stood up, 'Perhaps you would like to back that up with a gun,' he challenged Wallace.

'I don't carry a gun but I'll fight you, any time.' The crowd moved away giving Wallace plenty of room. 'Well, what do you say, gambling man?' The big miner knew that Jenks would not risk losing face fighting him. The gambler also knew that if it came to a fist-fight he would be in trouble against Wallace.

Tobias's voice broke the tension. 'If you want to stay in Silver City clean up your game. If not, get out.'

Jenks rounded on Tobias. This was his chance to save his face and enhance his reputation. He knew he was good with a gun. He had beaten some well-known shooters. If he beat this Negro he could rule Silver City. Jenks went for his gun. It was coming level when Tobias fired. The bullet hit Jenks in the left eye. His head exploded, splattering Buckley, who was standing staring at Tobias open-mouthed. He had never witnessed such speed. Then the gun was turned on him.

Buckley raised his hands. 'Don't shoot,' he pleaded.

'Take his gun, Pat, and lock him up. Silver City has a new marshal.'

## SIX

The clean-up of Silver City began. Jim Buckley was the first to be kicked out. Others soon followed. If any new faces were on the 'Wanted' posters, they were allowed a meal and care for their horses before being sent on their way. Bill Campbell was up and about and talking of moving on. Buffalo meat was in demand at a lot of railway camps and he wanted to make a load of money before he got too old. A railway delegation was due in soon to plan a route into Silver City. The mayor sent for Tobias and Flynn to meet them when they arrived. Both railway men, Ray Scott and Dan Brannan, spoke with a southern accent. When introduced to Tobias, their attitude changed noticeably. During the conversation both men ignored him. Pat Flynn felt their animosity towards his friend. Rising, he excused himself and Tobias and they left the mayor on his own to make any future plans for the proposed incoming railroad.

It was Ray Scott, the younger of the delegates, who angrily addressed the mayor. 'You didn't say you had a bloody black marshal.'

Outside, the two lawmen heard his raised voice. Flynn was stopped from going back inside by Tobias. 'Don't, Pat. Leave it.' The big lawman pulled his furious friend away from the door.

'It won't matter what colour you are if they run into trouble,' Flynn said, as they made their way back to the marshal's office.

The mayor was taken aback at Ray Scott's attitude. 'He's an excellent lawman. He's cleaned this town up,' he said in defence of his man.

'We have a lot of blacks working for us, laying tracks, and we have to keep them in their place. When they get here and see a Negro running this town they might get ideas above their station. Get rid of him.' Dan Brannan nodded in agreement with his partner's outburst. After further talks about land and routes into town they left. As they passed the marshal's office, Tobias stood watching from the doorway. Scott looked at him, contempt etched on his face. Tobias knew then that if he stayed on trouble was inevitable.

As the railroad came nearer the workers came into Silver City to drink and gamble and visit the brothel. With the help of Flynn and Bill Campbell, who had decided to stay on as a deputy, Tobias kept a quiet town.

A shot in the Main Chance saloon had Campbell striding through the doors, his big buffalo gun steady in his hands. A cowboy from one of the ranches outside of town stood with a gun in his hand. At his feet lay a body. 'What's going on here?'

The cowhand turned at the sound of the deputy's voice. 'He grabbed my girl as she passed.' The girl, who worked in the saloon, nodded her head in support of the cowboy's accusation. 'I don't want a black man mauling my girl,' he continued.

Tobias entered as he spoke. At the sight of him the cowboy pointed his gun at Tobias. The marshal drew and fired, the bullet hitting the young cowhand in the chest, knocking him over. Tobias's gun covered the crowded saloon as Bill Campbell knelt down to examine the two men lying on the floor. The cowhand was still alive.

'Get him to the Doc's. He's still breathing,' Campbell ordered, before turning his attention to the other body. He was a black railway worker. He lay dead, his overalls soaked in blood. Tobias stood looking down at him. It was evident to him and to everyone in the room that he was unarmed.

'What happened here?' Tobias asked, his eyes searching the faces of the silent crowd.

'He was pestering the girl. He got what he asked for,' a voice from the back called out adding, as an afterthought, 'Bloody nigger.'

Silence returned. Tobias looked around. The faces of *strangers* stared back at him. Some showing fear, others detestation. George Tobias felt alienated. Campbell touched his arm. His gesture was ignored and he stooped down and picked up the body of the dead railway worker. No help was offered. Most heads turned away as Tobias carried him out of the saloon and down the street to the undertaker's. Arriving there he kicked the door till it was opened. On entering, he placed the body on the first table he came to. Turning to the startled undertaker, he proffered a handful of silver dollars,

'Will that give him a decent funeral, with a coffin and a headstone?' he asked.

A barely audible 'Yes' was the undertaker's reply.

Tobias went outside, where Campbell was waiting for him. 'The cowhand will be OK. The doc's working on him now,' Campbell informed him.

'Put him in a cell when he can be moved,' Tobias told him, 'He will be tried for murder.' The deputy seemed hesitant. 'What's wrong Bill? Is there a problem?'

The old buffalo hunter looked embarrassed. 'You won't get a jury, never mind a verdict, son,' was Campbell's answer, 'Even if the district judge agrees to try him, a white man killing a Negro is just like killing an Indian, and you know what they say about Indians: the only good Indian is a dead one.' The silence which followed this statement was a long one.

'What will happen, Bill, when the railway gets closer and more black workers come into town? How am I supposed to behave? One law for the white man and another for the black? Where's the justice in that?'

The reasoning of the young marshal had Campbell stuck for words. Had Tobias been a white man he would probably have had little trouble convincing him that Indians and blacks came a poor second to whites in any dispute.

Marshal George Tobias made his way to

his office, where Pat Flynn was sorting a stack of "Wanted" posters. Workmen were building new cells at the back of the jailhouse to accommodate any future influx of law-breakers.

'What was all the shooting about, son?'

Tobias sat down before answering the question. Flynn listened as he recounted the events of the last few hours and of his talk with Bill Campbell. After a short pause, he continued, 'I know in the South, before the war, black people were treated badly but things should have improved a bit by now. We came out of the army because of the way the Indians were being rounded-up and abused by the authorities. Surely, with the coming of the settlers, who have also known hardship, things should be better?'

'Things take time to settle, son. We have to get used to each other's ways. People are suspicious of each other. Some use violence because they are violent people; others use it when they are frightened. Our job is to keep order till the day black and white and yellow and red can all live together in peace.'

Tobias shook his head. 'That black worker was left on the floor, Pat, and when that cowhand turned on me, nobody did anything to stop him. I'm wondering now what would have happened to him if he had shot me – another black man. My colour will be a hindrance, Pat. It will be an excuse to shoot at me and if they hit me it won't matter. Only my speed with a gun has saved me so far. People look up to me because of it but if I lose that ability, Pat, I'll be just another nigger.'

Flynn listened to his friend talk. He could see that what had happened out there tonight had upset him. If it had been Wyatt Earp or a white marshal, they would be buying drinks and slapping him on the back. He also knew that with the railway coming in, and more Southern folk mixing in the community, the feelings towards a black lawman would be prejudicial.

Tobias rose up from his chair. 'I'm going to Miss Elly's ranch. Tomorrow, I'm seeing the mayor.' Flynn made to go with him. 'No. Stay on a bit longer, Pat; I'll see you later.' He left as Bill Campbell came in.

Mano was in bed when Tobias rode in from town. Stabling his horse he entered the bunkhouse. Undressing wearily, he got into his bunk and slept, putting the events of the day out of his mind.

The two deputies stayed in town that night. They were up and about next morning, when Tobias rode in. His big frame filled the doorway; his dark shadow, falling across the desk, made Flynn look up at him. He knew, before Tobias spoke, what he was going to say. 'I'm handing in my badge, Pat. I've decided I'm the wrong colour.'

'Don't be put off by a few idiots,' the Irishman began. Tobias turned on his heels, ignoring his old sergeant, and made his way to the mayor's office to tell him his decision. Pat Flynn caught him up as a bunch of cavalry entered town, escorting a buckboard, occupied by Scott and Brannan, the two railway officials.

'Marshal,' Scott shouted as he pulled on the reins. Tobias and Flynn stood and watched as the horse soldiers halted and their captain dismounted to join the two railway officials. 'This is Captain Marks, marshal.' The disdain was evident in Scott's voice, as he continued, 'I have asked the army to bring in Federal law because we are not happy with what is going on in Silver City. The railway has a lot of money and men to look after. I believe we lost one of our workers last night – shot down in cold blood.'

The captain stepped in front of Scott effectively silencing him. 'Marshal.' He offered his hand to Tobias. 'We have ridden in with Scott because we are in this area, checking on Indian activity and he has asked us to come in and see if we can help you in any way.'

Scott resented being interrupted. He turned and with Brannan in tow he went in the direction of the mayor's office. Captain Marks let him go without comment. He looked at Tobias, waiting for his reply.

'There was a shooting in town last night. A black railworker was killed. The man who killed him was shot by me. He is in the doctor's house now, being attended to. He will be tried as soon as he's fit.'

'It sounds as if you don't need our help then, Marshal.'

'We don't,' Flynn broke in. 'It's Scott and his Southern upbringing that need help.'

The seasoned soldier made no comment, excused himself and took his men off in search of food and drink.

Tobias and Flynn entered the mayor's office as the railway officials were heatedly voicing their opinions. 'I have a couple of good men who can take the Negro's place,' Scott was stressing. Tobias took off his badge and threw it on the desk.

'Give that to whoever you please.'

Pat Flynn put his alongside, 'And mine as

well.' Then he took hold of Scott by his shirt front, 'You and your Southern bigotry will cause a lot of grief for you and your railway if you don't change your attitude.' Flynn slammed Scott down, into a chair. 'And you, Mr Mayor, if you can't tell the railmen what to do you shouldn't be in this job.'

Once outside, Flynn – still fuming – led the way to the office, where they found Captain Marks asking Bill Campbell questions about Tobias. Flynn was further outraged but, before he could say anything, Tobias quietened him. 'Captain, if you have anything on your mind, regarding myself, just ask. I'll be only too pleased to answer any accusations that may have been levelled at me.' His speech surprised the cavalry officer.

'Mr Campbell has already filled me in with the details of the shooting, thank you, Mr Tobias. As you can appreciate, this is a very sensitive and provoking situation and I'm not convinced that having a black marshal is a good idea.'

'I think Mr Scott has hoodwinked you, sir. Perhaps his hatred for black men is beginning to colour your vision.'

The captain began to protest but Tobias cut him short. 'Let me alone, Captain, or you will find yourself in deep trouble. I'm getting tired of saving white folk. From now on it's George Tobias first and last.'

Tobias left town after calling on Miss Elly. Pat Flynn caught up with him along the trail. He passed on Bill Campbell's best wishes and the news that he too had decided to leave. In his own words he was off to chase the buffalo. They were less ornery than folk. Silver City would, once again, be without a marshal.

The weeks went by with the two friends busy working on the two ranches. Miss Elly had improved tremendously. She seemed to be putting her ordeal behind her now. The day came when she returned to her ranch. Mano was overjoyed when Pat Flynn brought her home in the buckboard. It did not take long for her to settle in; Tobias and Flynn saw to that. They were there most days, helping her and Mano with the daily chores. The news from Silver City was that the rail bosses had brought in their own man to act as marshal – a man named Dave Sands – who had been a trouble-shooter for the railway.

Tobias went to town with Elly on the milk run. After making their deliveries they went to see the doctor so that he could check on Elly's progress. He told Tobias that the white ranch hand he had shot, for killing the black railway worker, had been set free without a trial and that lawlessness was once more rife in the town. There were regular fights between miners and railway workers. The new sheriff was coming down hard on the miners, fining them on the spot or else jailing them for seven days. These were options the miners could ill afford. The fines were steep but if they went to jail their claim would be forfeit. Claim jumpers were only too eager to move in and work their diggings once they had been left unmanned.

Tobias shook his head but there was worse to come. The doctor told him that Jim Buckley had returned to Silver City and was now a deputy. Tobias decided that it was time for him to leave town before Buckley came looking for him. He did not want any shooting in front of Elly. They said their farewells and climbed aboard. As he was turning the cart, a buckboard pulled alongside. Ray Scott was pulling on the reins. Tobias sat still, waiting for the reason for his action.

'Miss Elly Morgan isn't it?' Scott took off his hat as he spoke. Dan Brannan sat uneasily beside him, eyeing Tobias. Arrogantly ignoring Tobias, Scott addressed Elly, 'We would like to buy your spread. When I say we I mean the railway. We would be willing to pay a good price.'

Tobias kept silent. It was nothing to do with him. It was her land and if she wanted to sell it it was up to her.

Scott continued, 'The railway is moving further south. Going through your land would save us a long detour.'

Elly grasped Tobias's hand. 'We will talk it over and let you know,' she replied.

Scott flushed. 'What's it got to do with him? You don't live with that nigger do you?'

Tobias kept his temper under control. He could see that Elly was starting to get upset. 'Move out of the way, railwayman.' Tobias's hand dropped to his gun as he spoke.

Scott hesitated then moved away slowly. 'Let me know, lady, if you want to sell and don't leave it too late.' With that, he whipped his horse in the direction of the marshal's office.

A week later the buckboard pulled up outside Elly's ranch. Two men got down and made their way to the front porch. Mano ran to tell Tobias. '*Señor*, quick. Two men call.' Tobias followed the excited Mexican back to the porch, in time to see two men knock at the door. He recognized Ray Scott. The other was a stranger: a tall, lean man,

110

dressed all in black, with a gun on his right hip. He turned and looked about as Scott continued to knock loudly on the door. His marshal's badge reflected in the sunlight. So this was Dave Sands, Tobias thought, as he approached the pair. Scott removed his hat, when Elly, looking as lovely as ever, came to the door. Sands, completely ignoring her, was watching the big Negro. This was the first time he had seen Tobias. Jim Buckley had warned him how fast he was and how he had out-drawn and shot Lew Jenks and now, seeing him, he knew it would be dangerous to get involved with him. Sands stepped back as Tobias climbed the few steps to the porch door. Scott was annoyed at the sight of him. He was hoping to talk to Elly alone.

'Do you need me, Miss Elly?' Tobias asked.

'Yes, I would be glad if you would stay to hear what Mr Scott has to say. He won't be staying long.'

It was evident to Scott that his visit was going to be a waste of time. 'I have been sent by my bosses to make you an offer of double the price of what this place is worth...'

'I'm sorry,' Elly cut in, 'I have no intention of selling to you or anyone else.' She turned to re-enter the house when Scott's outburst stopped her.

'I should also inform you of the trouble a lot of ranchers are having with Indian raids. A lot of stock is being stolen. Ranches are being burned and their owners butchered. Their womenfolk are being raped and scalped ... I believe you know something of rape and its effects.'

The smirk on his face turned to shock as Tobias grabbed him and hurled him bodily from the porch. Dave Sands automatically went for his gun. Tobias pounced. His left hand clamped on Sands' gun, his right hand dipped to his boot. The knife came out and only Elly's scream saved Sands from being gutted. The shaken lawman fell back as Tobias took his gun and threw it into the buckboard.

'Don't cross me again. If you do...' His threat was left unfinished. He turned his back on them, contemptuously, as they scrambled into the buckboard and rode away.

Elly was leaning against the door, sobs racking her body. Tobias stood helplessly by. He wanted to take her in his arms, touch her, comfort her. He did not know what to do. He cursed his uselessness. His great strength and fitness was no use to him in a situation like this. It was Mano who helped her. His gentle manner and soft voice soothed her, as he guided her back into the house. Tobias followed them in. The rattle of wheels jogged Tobias back to reality. Thinking it was Scott and the marshal returning he went to the door. He was relieved to see it was Pat Flynn returning from the milk run.

'What's happened, son? I've just passed Scott and the new marshal heading back to town.' Tobias told him. 'How's Elly taking it?' Flynn asked.

'Not too good, Pat. I thought she'd settled but as soon as Scott mentioned the Indian attacks and rape she just broke down and I didn't help any by losing my temper.'

'You know, one thing puzzles me about these Indian attacks, Captain Marks says no arrows were found at the last raid. Anyway, let's see how Elly is.' He followed Tobias into the ranch-house. Mano had made coffee. The strong, hot drink settled Elly and Flynn told Mano to stay with her while they went to check on their own ranch. Everything was going well under Hank Jay's management. He had not seen any Indians about but agreed to warn the men to be extra vigilant when Tobias told him of the rumours that were being circulated in the town.

It was dusk when they set off back to Elly's ranch. The sound of gunfire had them spurring their mounts forward. Then their way was lit by an explosion of red flames. Fear for the safety of Elly Morgan and Mano had them driving their horses to their limit. Arriving at the ranch their worst fears were realized. They found Mano's body lying face down on the steps of the porch. The flames licked hungrily about him as Tobias ran up the steps with Flynn alongside him. They picked him up and moved him away from the blazing ranch-house. He was dead: shot in the back. Tobias ran back shouting Elly's name. The flames, roaring through the house drove him back. Flynn joined him in his search. The pungent smell of burning oil rose in the air as they ran round the building trying to find a way in. Both men gave up all hope as one side of the building collapsed. It took all of Flynn's strength to stop Tobias from going into the raging inferno. In a vain hope that Elly was still alive they frantically searched the outbuildings. But there was no sign of her. As the final part of the ranch crumbled in flames, Flynn and Tobias tore at the blazing wood in their frantic search for Elly. It was Flynn who found the charred body. The flames flared and died and the sparks burned them as they tossed the burning debris aside. Elly Morgan's body was lifted by Tobias as Flynn ran to the bunk-house for a blanket. She was lying down, alongside Mano, when Flynn returned to find Tobias cradling her head in his arms, his giant frame shaking.

'Why Pat? Who would want to do such a thing? She harmed nobody.' Flynn could not answer him but he knew that whoever it was who had done this would pay with their lives. They wrapped both of the bodies in blankets and took them into Silver City.

The milk wagon pulled up outside the marshal's office. Flynn jumped down. The night deputy told him he would find Sands in the hotel. Pat Flynn left Tobias with the bodies as he went to raise him. Sands was with Buckley and Ray Scott, drinking in his room, when Flynn knocked. His smoked and burnt appearance startled the marshal when he opened the door. Flynn pushed his way in. When he saw who he was with he was taken aback. A bottle of whiskey was open on the table in the room. Buckley and Scott, glasses in their hands were startled at Flynn's intrusion.

'While you are here drinking,' Flynn shouted, 'people are being burned out and murdered. Elly Morgan's ranch was burned down tonight. Both she and Mano are dead.'

'Well, didn't we warn you about the Indian raiding parties?' Scott said, 'The marshal can't do anything. It's a job for the army.' He drank his whiskey. 'How about her black friend? Couldn't he chase them away?'

If Dave Sands had not grabbed Pat Flynn and offered to go with him to see the bodies he would have killed Ray Scott there and then. Sands told Tobias how sorry he was about the two deaths. He assured him that at first light he would be out looking for clues and that the army would be informed as soon as possible.

Tobias remained silent, too distressed to say anything. He sat with Elly all night in the undertaker's. He was still there the next morning when the doctor inspected the bodies. Both had been shot.

The marshal was informed and, along with Jim Buckley, Captain Marks and his troop, they all set off together to look around the burnt-out shell of the ranch-house. There was no sign of any big Indian war party. A number of .45 shells were found but nothing else. Captain Marks's patrol left to search the surrounding territory and Sands and his deputy returned to town. Tobias and Flynn took Elly's herd to their own ranch till something could be sorted out legally. Then they went back to town for the burial service, before returning to their own spread.

Next day, Tobias was putting a couple of boxes of ammunition into his saddle-bags when Flynn came back from a check-up of Elly's stock. Before Flynn could question him about his intentions Tobias told him he was going to see Big Eagle about the suspected Indian raids, to see if he could shed any light on the matter. Tobias halted Flynn's protest by turning his back, mounting his horse and riding away. He spurred his mount forward. He would find Big Eagle, get his revenge and ride on. That was if he came out of it alive.

## SEVEN

Tobias made for the area where he had found Nahita. That night he set up camp and after eating a meal, settled down to sleep. At dawn, a faint sound awoke him. The sight of moccasins and the buffalo-hide trousers pleased him. Her people had found him. He stood up feeling no fear. One of them had his pistol. 'Come,' he demanded.

117

Tobias made ready and mounted his horse. The Indians' ponies encircled him and they headed towards a low mountain range in the distance where they followed a twisting and winding trail upwards and then down. They passed a guard, who seemed to appear from nowhere only to vanish in the same direction. A number of wigwams came into view. A smokeless fire was burning and women were busy preparing a meal. As they entered, one of them ran to a large wigwam shouting a warning. Big Eagle came out and approached Tobias, a look of recognition and pleasure on his face. The leader of the party spoke to his chief then handed him Tobias's gun. Big Eagle returned the pistol to Tobias and motioned for him to dismount and follow him. On entering the wigwam, Tobias was pleased to find Nahita there. It was evident that she was with child. Placing his pistol before him on the ground, he sat cross-legged, facing the chief. His action puzzled Big Eagle and he spoke in Sioux to his daughter.

'You are troubled. What is wrong?' Nahita asked.

'A number of ranches have been raided and burnt recently, and Indians are being blamed. I lost some close friends two nights ago.'

Big Eagle listened as Tobias answered his daughter's questions. He understood some of what was said. 'No. White men from big iron horse do this.' The chief angrily defended his tribe. Nahita translated her father's words. While skirting the area near Elly's ranch, members of their tribe had witnessed the attack and then followed the raiders back to the railway camp, near Silver City.

At first Tobias found it difficult to believe what the chief had said, then the truth of the matter slowly sank in. He recalled Scott's venomous words the fatal day he had visited the ranch with his offer. If what the chief said was true he would have to get in touch with Captain Marks.

Tobias told them about the army search party while they ate the food that Nahita brought to them. Big Eagle already knew that the patrol was active. There had been recent skirmishes with his braves, a number of whom had been killed. That was why they had moved to a safer camp in the mountains. Big Eagle left the wigwam to talk to his men, leaving Tobias alone with Nahita. She came close to him. Taking his hand, she placed it on her swollen stomach. Tobias could feel the unborn child moving.

'Soon, baby son for Nahita. His name

Tobias like his father.' She smiled when she realized that what she had said had surprised him. The big Negro's arm went round her shoulders. Her soft warm body brought back the memories of the pleasure he had experienced that night at the camp-fire. Tobias knew that it was his son that she carried.

Big Eagle entered the wigwam to find them locked in an embrace. Tobias asked him, through Nahita, if he would allow his daughter to marry him. The chief was pleased for Nahita to be betrothed to Tobias, whom he saw as a warrior of great courage, and told him to go away and return in four days, when all the arrangements befitting a chief's daughter would be completed. Tobias was escorted back along the trail that led out of the mountains.

Pat Flynn was surprised to see the big rider emerge out of the darkness as he made his rounds of the ranch and its buildings. It was a routine he followed every night, now, since Elly Morgan's ranch had been razed to the ground. His rifle came up. The rider halted.

'Is that you, Sergeant Flynn?'

Pat Flynn ran to meet Tobias as he dismounted. 'I thought you had gone for good, son.' His big arms went around Tobias as he welcomed him back. 'Where have you been?'

Tobias told him of his meeting with the Sioux and what Big Eagle had said about the raid on Elly's spread. 'You see, Pat, if it wasn't Indians, there's only the railway who would benefit from the destruction of the ranch. If I remember, it was Scott who blamed the Indians and who called the army in. That's why I have come back. Tomorrow I'm going to face Scott to see what he has to say for himself.'

They entered the ranch-house where Tobias told Flynn more about his encounter with Big Eagle and of his plans to marry Nahita.

'You do what you want, son. It might settle you down and this place needs a woman.' Flynn got up and retired for the night, leaving Tobias with his thoughts about the morrow.

Next morning they both rode out. They had decided to confront the mayor and then Dave Sands. After all, as Flynn said, he had once been employed by the railway as a troubleshooter. Dismounting outside the mayor's office, they knocked and entered. When he saw who his visitors were the mayor became decidedly uncomfortable. Tobias told him of his conversation with the Indians.

'You don't believe what an Indian tells you, do you?'

The mayor's remark angered Tobias. 'Yes, I do, and I'll tell you this, if I find what they say is true, you won't need a judge or jury.'

They left the mayor's office and searched Silver City. There was no sign of the marshal or his deputy. They decided to try the rail camp. As they approached the railhead, Tobias remained cool. Pat Flynn watched him. He knew that if Scott was there, Tobias would kill him and anyone else who got in his way. The site was a hive of industry; rail-lines were being laid; a steam engine was noisily shunting a flat-bed wagon bringing up the wooden sleepers and iron pins. An office shed stood back away from the noise and activity. Outside was a buckboard and two saddle-horses. Tobias made his way towards the shack. Just then, Jim Buckley came out, spotted Flynn and Tobias and turned back inside. Ray Scott emerged with Buckley and the marshal on either side of him. Tobias stopped and dismounted. Flynn remained in his saddle.

A number of men had ceased working at the sight of the giant Negro. His notoriety had spread among them but many had never set eyes on him. Now, curiosity got the better of them. They stood and watched as the black man confronted the three men. They saw him speak to Scott and then Scott point angrily at Tobias. The hand was knocked down and then both the marshal and deputy went for their guns. They saw Tobias's hand drop and lift. The two shots sounded almost simultaneously. Both lawmen fell back. Then Scott turned to run back into his office. He stopped in his tracks as Tobias grabbed him. He screamed as he was pulled back off his feet. The gun hit him on the head. The sound could be heard by the workers, as they stood and watched. Fear, at the fury of the black giant, rooted them to the spot, as he rained blows down on the crumbling Scott.

Flynn jumped from his horse and grabbed at his young friend, only to be shaken off as Tobias's frenzy increased. The screaming ended and the limp body was thrown to one side where it lay motionless.

Tobias shouted to the railway workers. 'Where's Brannan?' A worker pointed to the office. Tobias stormed through the door and dragged the cowering Brannan outside.

'It wasn't me. I didn't do anything. It was Scott, with the marshal and his deputy who raided the girl's ranch.'

Flynn aimed his rifle at his friend. 'Let him go, son. There's been enough killing.' Tobias put Brannan between them, all his reasoning had left him. He wanted total revenge on Elly's killers and this was the last one. He put his gun to the back of Brannan's head and pulled the trigger. The lifeless body fell from his grasp. The railway workers drew back at the cold-blooded killing. Tobias faced Flynn, whose rifle was still pointing at this body. He put his gun back in its holster.

'Shoot the black bastard,' a voice called out, as the workers moved forward, threateningly.

Tobias pushed Flynn's rifle to one side and faced them with no sign of fear. 'This "black bastard" has three bullets left in his gun. Which three of you wants to die?' He stood waiting, his face a twisted mask. No one responded. He mounted his horse and turned in the saddle to address his old sergeant. 'Goodbye Pat.'

With that, he spurred his horse and rode away. He could see the mountains in the distance. A wife and son waited there for him. His spurs touched the horse. It increased its pace. The young Negro settled in his saddle. He would miss his old sergeant but he knew that if he stayed with Pat he would only bring him trouble. The mountains came nearer as his horse ate up the ground. His pace slackened as he followed the climbing trail and he was puzzled to find that there was no sign of a look-out. Tobias knew he would get lost if he ventured further without a guide. Dismounting, he began to walk. A moan, to the right of him, brought his gun to his hand. Moving silently, he came upon the look-out, lying face down, a knife protruding from his side. Tobias bent down to see how bad the wound was. The knife was well embedded. The Indian watched him as he made a pad, then held his breath as the blade was pulled from his flesh. The pad was pressed and bound tightly to the bleeding wound. As gently as he could, Tobias helped the Indian on to his horse, then gestured for him to point out the way to the camp. With Tobias on foot they set off.

The Indian was weakening. The blood was running through his fingers as the pad became soaked. Tobias was worried. Somebody should have met them by now. They came into the clearing and Tobias was stopped in his tracks by what he saw. There had been a massacre: bodies lay everywhere; men, women and children had been shot and left to die. The Indian brave slid off the horse. Tobias caught him and laid him on the ground. He was dead.

The big Negro walked round, looking for signs of life. Big Eagle lay outside his wigwam; a bullet to the head had killed him. Nahita lay close by. Her hands, covered in blood, were clutching her stomach. He lifted her up into his arms and as he did so a faint moan escaped her lips. She was still warm: she was still alive. He placed her gently back down on the ground and cut at her dress to inspect where she had been shot, but there were no bullet wounds. A dead foetus lay between her thighs. The baby, their son, was dead. As she became aware of him, Nahita told Tobias what to do. The young Negro followed her instructions silently and competently. He made her more comfortable and helped her into the wigwam. All this was done in the eerie silence that pervaded the stricken camp.

As the numbness subsided they began to go over the tragic events. Nahita told Tobias about the massacre. There had been a volley of shots from the surrounding rocks. Nobody had stood a chance.

'Did you see who they were?' asked Tobias.

'Yankee soldiers,' she said. Tobias could not believe it. He knew Captain Marks had his men out, rounding up Indians, but not murdering them, like this. What if they came back? They would be safer away from the camp. They decided to take Big Eagle and their baby son to the high ground and between them, would perform the burial ceremony.

Tobias laid the blanket-shrouded body of the Sioux chief across his horse. Nahita, cradling her tiny bundle, silently rose and followed as he led the laden horse along the track that took them higher into the mountains.

Once the ceremony was completed they made a new camp where they stayed until Nahita was well enough to travel. While she was recovering, Tobias familiarized himself with the trails that crisscrossed the mountains. He went through his old training routine daily. Another week passed. Nahita stood watching him practising his knife throwing. She saw him pull the knife from his boot, turn and throw. It flew straight to the target he had built.

'I show Tobias how to fight with knife, Indian way.'

He was amazed at what she taught him. He learnt quickly and well.

Days later, the Negro and the Indian squaw rode out. Tobias had wanted to wait a while longer to aid Nahita's recovery but she wanted to get on the trail of the horse soldiers before they left the area for new pastures. Nahita, with her tracking skills, led the way. Tobias followed quietly, not questioning. When they were hungry, she would trap an animal, they would eat and off they would go again.

On the evening of the second day, she stopped suddenly and dismounted, handing her pony over to Tobias. 'You stay,' she said and then vanished into the dusk that was now falling. Tobias sat waiting, getting edgy, as the time passed. The small shadowy figure appeared silently beside him. His gun was in his hand and cocked. 'Tobias.' The voice stopped his trigger-finger before it fired the gun. 'We wait here short time. Then go see pony soldiers.'

Tobias knew she must have found what she had been searching for. She leaned on his chest. His hand stroked her hair. Tobias felt at ease with her. There seemed to be a bond holding them together.

He wondered what Pat Flynn was doing now. His thoughts travelled back. Pat had heard Scott and the two lawmen admit to the burning of Elly's ranch. Tobias went over the conversation that led up to shoot-out. They had scoffed at him thinking they could take him – three against one – but they had under-estimated him. He had killed them because he knew nobody would have believed him. What had they called him? A black bastard. Well, Pat Flynn was white; perhaps the townspeople would believe him. The workers, too, had heard Brannan admit it was Scott who had organized the ranch raids.

Nahita's movement broke into his thoughts. 'We go now,' she said as she led Tobias into the night. Her shuffling gait slowed as the silhouettes of two tents came into view. They crouched as a sentry coughed. He stood looking about and then turned to walk away. Tobias was up, his knife ready. He pushed it into the sentry's back, all his massive strength behind it. His other hand was cupped over the sentry's mouth, pulling back on his head. The rifle fell from his lifeless fingers. The two silent figures eased their way closer to the nearest tent. Nahita stooped, a knife in her hand. The razor-sharp blade cut into the canvas. She peered through the slit, her keen eyes searching the murky interior. Four shapes lay huddled in their blankets. Her knife slid further down. The gap in the canvas widened. She stepped into the tent, with

Tobias close behind, his knife in his right hand. Nahita moved to the left. Tobias went to the right, both stepping silently between the sleepers.

A slim brown hand went over the first soldier's mouth. The knife cut gently. It slid from left to right. The body twitched, then lay still. Nahita moved to the next sleeper. He turned, disturbed. Nahita stood silent. He settled again. Still. The point of her knife stopped two inches from the sleeper's throat. His eyes opened. Then she thrust the knife deep into his Adam's apple. His mouth opened to scream. It was silenced as the blood choked off the sound. The knife was driven deeper by the squaw, who had seen her father and tribe wiped out. Then he died, not knowing what had happened to him.

On the other side of the tent Tobias had done the same, not caring or showing any feelings at all. He stood upright now, looking at the four corpses. Then he followed Nahita to the next tent. This time they would walk into the tent through the front entrance. There was now no need to be quiet. They knew that there would not be any more than six men in the tent. Tobias put his knife back into his boot and took out his gun. Nahita was first into the tent. The first man died with his throat cut. This time there was no need for silence. She turned as the next soldier woke with a start, his shout rousing his companions. Tobias's gun barked its death-knell. They left one alive in his bed-roll.

'Where's Captain Marks?' Tobias demanded. The horse soldier, fearing for his life, told Tobias Captain Marks had gone to Silver City to keep law and order until a new lawman could be appointed.

'Was your patrol responsible for the massacre of the Indians in the mountains, Silver City way?'

The trooper began to splutter. 'We were following the captain's orders.' Tobias shot him, then turned away and left the tent. If Captain Marks was in Silver City, that was their next stop and the man who had been responsible for their baby son's death would soon pay with his own. They moved away from the scene of death, made camp and slept wrapped together.

# EIGHT

A month had gone by since Pat Flynn had watched Tobias climb aboard his horse and ride away. He had loved him as a son and had seen him grow up, from a gangly loose-limbed youngster into a fine young man, anyone would have been proud of. Now he had been turned into a killing machine. He had been called 'nigger' and 'black bastard'. He had tried, unsuccessfully, to settle and live in a white man's world. If he had been white, the population of Silver City would have hero-worshipped him. He had just killed four killers but if the crowd at the railhead could have got hold of him, Flynn knew they would have strung him up. He felt himself partly to blame. He should have taken him away from Silver City after winning the shooting and boxing contests. He hoped Tobias would return home. Now, all he could do was sit and wait. Flynn kept himself busy on the ranch.

After the shooting at the railhead, there had been an enquiry by the top bosses of the railway. It turned out that Scott had been responsible for the burning of certain ranches and the killing of the owners, who would not sell or give permission for the railway's progress through their land. He would then buy up the land, at a low rate, and sell it to the railway company, under an assumed name, at a higher price. It was decided that no charges were to be brought against Tobias for the killings.

That night, a knock on the door roused Flynn. He did what he always did when anybody called late. He picked up his rifle and opened the door. The change in the appearance of the man he saw standing before him was frightening. The face was leaner. The eyes had a stare of mistrust, a hardness, now, that had not been there before.

'Hello, Pat.'

Even the voice had an edge to it. It was as if he was challenging you. A slight figure stood alongside him. This would be Nahita, thought Flynn. There was a wildness about her Indian beauty. With her hair bound in thick plaits and her eyes darkly piercing she exuded a proud confidence. The Irishman, for once, was stuck for words.

'Are you letting us in?' Tobias broke into his thoughts.

'Yes. Come in son.' Flynn stood to one side as Tobias let Nahita go before him, and pushed her gently into the house. Tobias knew that Flynn would make them welcome. He also knew that Flynn could see a change in him. There had always been a bond between them but now, all the recent events had changed Tobias and he had a feeling that Flynn did not like what he saw.

'Sit down, son, and I will make you something to eat and then we can talk.'

Tobias made Nahita comfortable and then followed Pat Flynn into the kitchen. The young giant stood and watched him while he prepared the food, before starting a conversation.

'I've come back to kill Captain Marks.' Before he could say anything else, Flynn spun round at him.

'What?' Flynn was shocked. He could not believe what he was hearing. 'You can't go on killing people. And why the captain?'

Tobias told him about the Indian massacre and of his son's death and of the revenge killing of the cavalry patrol. Flynn was dumbfounded. Then he took Tobias by the shoulders.

'Son. You've got to stop this. You're starting to enjoy killing. When you killed Scott and his crew, I watched you. If I had tried to stop you, you would have killed me, too. Up until now, you have been lucky. You have got away with it. The railway enquiry decided not to bring charges against you but you can't kill Marks. He's Army and following government orders.'

Tobias shook Flynn off. 'They can't get away with murder and I aim to repay them,' he replied.

'You should let the law see to it, son. You can't avenge everybody's death.' Sadness was in Flynn's voice.

Tobias went back to Nahita. 'We will eat here and move on.' She nodded in agreement. Nahita had heard the raised voices and knew, from the bits of the conversation she understood, that Flynn wanted Tobias to stay and settle but she was pleased that Tobias, like her, wanted revenge. When they had found Captain Marks and killed him, only then would her father's and their son's spirits rest in the happy hunting grounds. They took the food that Pat Flynn offered them and ate it silently.

'We could sell out and move up north to the northern cities. We could get into the fight game son, and make a good living,' Flynn's voice pleaded. Tobias was tempted.

Nahita watched him. She knew Tobias's friendship for Flynn was very strong. She rose up. 'You stay. I go.'

'No.' Tobias rose with her. 'It won't work, Pat. I'm the wrong colour.' He took Nahita's hand. 'We both are.'

'Wait a minute, son.' Flynn opened a cupboard in the corner of the room. He came back with a money belt. 'Here, take this. It's your share of the ranch's profit and if you need any more, get in touch.' Tobias did not refuse the money. He put it under his shirt, took Pat's proffered hand and then left.

It was quiet in Silver City. Nearing the main street, they made their way to the rear of the marshal's office. Alongside the new cells that had been built was a lean-to for the horses. Inside were four mounts. The government brand, on their flanks, was proof enough that soldiers were keeping order in the town. Tobias watched as Nahita moved, like a shadow, round the outside of the office. She listened and stopped, searched and moved on. After a while she came back. She told him that the soldiers were sleeping in the back. Tobias knew then that they were probably using the cells for sleeping quarters. Getting some dry brushwood and anything else that would burn, they built it

136

round the front door of the office. No one was about in the early hours, as Tobias lit the fire. The dry tinder soon caught. He stood and watched as the flames built up. Then he moved round to the back of the building. Nahita was sitting on her pony, holding the reins of Tobias's horse. Tobias banged on the back door.

'Fire. Fire!' he shouted.

He heard the bolts being drawn. A dishevelled head appeared. Before he could ask any questions, Tobias met him shouting, 'Quick. The office is on fire. Get the prisoners out.'

'We have no prisoners.' His reply was cut short as the knife was plunged into his ribs, piercing his heart. His body was pushed to one side. Tobias entered the back door. He could smell smoke as he went forward. Captain Marks met him, a lighted oil-lamp in his grasp. Two men were close behind him.

'Thanks for the warning, fella.' The sight of the gun in the Negro's hand slowed his pace. The pistol exploded. The bullet hit the lamp, then entered the officer's chest. Flames ran up his arm as the oil from the lamp soaked his shirt. The other two soldiers collided with the burning officer. Tobias continued to shoot, emptying the rest of the gun into them. He then ran from the building, the front of which was well ablaze.

He leapt aboard his horse as voices could be heard in the street. He dug his spurs home and his horse surged forward. Nahita led the way. Her slight body lying flat on her pony's back.

Once they were clear of Silver City they slowed down. They could see the fire. It had not spread far. The townfolk must have got it under control. They moved on, this time at an energy-saving gait. There was a future ahead for them, now, and Tobias would see that nobody got in their way.

Pat Flynn was awakened from a restless night's sleep by the sound of hooves thundering into the yard of the ranch. Dawn was breaking as he opened the door to step into the yard, his rifle in his hands. A posse of town folk with a sprinkling of cavalry were milling about. Hank Jay, Flynn's ramrod, was questioning the riders as Flynn appeared on the scene.

'What's the problem?' Flynn enquired of his head man.

'It seems there was an Indian raid in the town last night. The marshal's office was set alight. Captain Marks and three of his men were shot and burned. The town is organizing a posse and they want you to lead them in a search for the Indians,' answered Jay.

'Why me?' Flynn asked as he turned to the townspeople.

'With you being an ex-deputy we thought you could lead us till an army officer arrives. If the Indians are still in the area we might be able to catch them.' It was the town mayor who answered Flynn's question.

Flynn's thoughts went back to the previous night and of his talk with Tobias; his talk of finding Captain Marks and of his revenge if he found him. Well, it looked as if he had.

'Give me a minute to get ready.' Flynn turned to Hank Jay, 'Keep an eye on the ranch till I get back. The Indians may be out looking for more places to raid.' Flynn went into the ranch-house to return almost immediately ready for the search. He knew that by now Tobias would be miles away with his squaw and if this search party found him he, Flynn, would be there to help him if the need arose.

The posse searched all day but no sign of any raiding party was found. What they did find was a flock of vultures circling and screeching as they dived from the sky to vanish below the horizon. Flynn led the posse to see what lay ahead, dreading what they were to find.

Two tents came into view. They could see the horses nibbling grass and moving about aimlessly. The vultures were entering the tents. Their screeching and the smell of death slowed the posse to a walk. Several stopped. It was Flynn who walked his horse on. He stopped when he found the sentry. The vultures had stripped the body clean before going into the tent to seek more carcasses. Flynn lifted his rifle and fired into the tents. The gorging vultures emerged from cover, the flesh and blood dripping from their beaks. They screamed defiance at the interruption of their meal. Flynn shot them as they appeared in view. Some flew to escape only to be blasted from the sky by Flynn's unerring aim. Only when the rifle ran out of bullets were the scavengers safe as they flew away screeching their defiance. Flynn remained seated as the posse came up behind him. The anger, that had engulfed his being at the sight that was before him, abated. He automatically loaded his rifle before dismounting and leading the men to peer into the tents.

Most of the posse had seen death before

but to see men, still in their beds – most with their throats cut – both shocked and angered them. Flynn stood and looked. How Tobias had changed – from an easy-going youth into a relentless killer. It was the mayor who broke into his thoughts.

'It might have been the same band of Indian savages who raided the town last night and killed Marks and his men.' Flynn's hostile stare made the town official step back in fear. For Flynn knew that it was the behaviour of people, such as the mayor, that was responsible for turning Tobias into what he had become. Flynn bit his tongue to stop himself uttering his bitter thoughts. 'Find a couple of spades and get this place cleaned up.' He barked the command as he left the tent, kicking at a dead vulture he had shot.

The camp was soon cleaned up. Holes were dug and everything, including the torn tents, was buried. The horses were rounded up and driven back to town. Pat Flynn was a tired man when he finally returned to his ranch. The townspeople were convinced that it had been Indians who had killed Captain Marks and his patrol. Only one man knew who the real killer was and that was Pat Flynn and that secret would go with him to his grave.

Months went by and the raid was forgotten. The ranch-work was now Pat Flynn's life but not a day went by without him thinking of George Tobias. He had his own cattle brand, the FT, which stood for Flynn and Tobias. He hoped one day that Tobias would return. Elly Morgan's ranch had been left to him and Tobias, a fact that came to light when Mr Cohen – a Silver City solicitor – returned from a trip to Chicago to hear of her death. He revealed that she had made a will leaving all her property and anything of value to Flynn and Tobias on condition that they kept Mano on with a job for life.

Flynn hired a Mexican and his wife to look after the milk herd which had been Elly's pride and joy. He also gave permission for the railroad to go through Elly's land as well as across the corner of his own spread. A considerable amount of money was deposited into his bank account, both for the right of way and for any inconvenience the railway was likely to cause.

Pat Flynn was now a man of means. He still rode out with his men. He also kept himself very fit working out regularly. His men sometimes joined him in his sparring sessions, one or two ending up with bloody noses. He taught his men to be more accurate when firing their rifles. He missed Tobias. The FT ranch was a thriving concern and so was Silver City. A new marshal had arrived by the name of Matthew Dillon and from all reports he was doing a very good job. Law and order had returned to the area. Indian parties were a rare sight in the surrounding district of Silver City. The railway had gone through and now telegraph lines were being put up in its wake.

Pat Flynn received a surprise visit from Wallace, the big miner who had been one of the boxing contenders in the tournament that had first brought Flynn and Tobias to Silver City. Wallace had with him a young man named James Elliot, who was a mining engineer. The silver was beginning to show signs of petering out on the face of the mountains and Wallace was convinced that there was plenty below ground. Elliot had tested certain areas and had confirmed what Wallace had suspected but money was the problem, so they decided to ask Flynn to join them in forming a Limited Mining Company. After talks the three men decided to venture into underground mining which proved a successful investment for Flynn. Money was soon pouring in from this new source and Pat Flynn was going to be a very rich man. However all the riches in the world could not make up for the loneliness he felt in his heart. A loneliness caused by the absence of George Tobias.

It was on one of those lonely nights that Flynn's thoughts were interrupted by the sound of a horse outside the ranch-house. The rattle of wheels and horse-harness had him taking up his rifle. He waited but no knock came to the door. Hearing a horse blowing and the stamping of hooves, Flynn dimmed the light before looking through the window. Outside was a covered wagon. A shape was slumped across the seat. Flynn cautiously opened the door.

'Hello,' he called as he approached the wagon. The figure on the seat remained motionless. Flynn looked across to the bunk-house to see if any of his crew had heard the wagon's approach. It was in darkness. He reached up to touch the still form. A low moan came from it at Flynn's touch. The big Irishman placed his rifle against the wagon and reached up. Realising something was wrong, he pulled the form down into his arms. There was no weight in it. The head fell against his shoulder. Long hair cascaded into his face. He took the woman into his house. She mumbled something about 'in the wagon'. Flynn laid her down and covered her with a blanket then lit an oil lamp and went to look in the wagon. A man's body lay there. He must have been dead a few days. Flynn picked up his rifle and re-entered his house. He checked on the woman then went and put some water on the stove to heat up. He made some coffee which he forced, as gently as he could, between her lips. This seemed to revive her a little. Then with some of the water he bathed her face. She opened her eyes and looked at Flynn. Her striking green eyes startled him. Her lips moved. A whispered 'Thank you' was barely audible. Then she said, 'Tom?'

'Rest now,' Flynn replied gently, as he made her more comfortable. Her eyes closed again. Tom must be the name of the man in the back of the wagon, thought Flynn as he stood looking down at her. She was a pretty woman even though her face was ashen white and drawn. A few wrinkles at the corner of her eyes put her age at around thirty. Women had not figured strongly in Flynn's life but suddenly he wanted to know more about this one. He sat in a comfortable chair, close to the sleeping woman. He decided he would stay there for the rest of the night. At the first light of day he would check the wagon and its contents.

Flynn slept lightly awakening at every movement of the sleeping woman. Eventually the sunlight woke him. His immediate concern was for the woman. Her green eyes were staring at him, a touch of fear in them. She watched as Flynn stood before her. She saw a big, rugged man, going grey, his eyes peering enquiringly at her with no sign of danger for her in them.

'Are you feeling better?' His soft Irish brogue settled her fears.

'Yes,' she replied, her voice stronger.

'You mentioned Tom, last night,' Flynn reminded her. 'There is a body in the wagon.' Tears began to run down her face as he reminded her.

'That's my husband Tom. He died the night before last. I think it was his appendix. He had terrible stomach pains and then he died. I got lost, then I saw your light and managed to turn the wagon in this direction.'

A frenzied knocking on the door interrupted her explanation.

'Pat.' It was Hank Jay. 'Do you know there's a wagon outside with a dead body in it?'

Flynn nodded an answer. 'Move it away.' He pointed to the wagon. 'Take the body out and lay it in the bunk-house. I'll explain later.' Flynn moved back inside the house, closing the door on more questions from his crew.

The woman was now standing waiting for Flynn's return. 'I will make some breakfast and then you can tell me all about it,' Flynn said.

'Thank you.' She had regained some kind of composure. 'My name's Fielding. Beth Fielding,' she told Flynn.

'I'm Pat Flynn. I own this ranch along with a man called George Tobias who is away just now.'

Flynn cooked the breakfast and watched the tall fair woman eat it with relish. When they had finished she told Pat that she and her husband Tom had come West to settle, from Chicago. He had been a bank teller and she had worked as a cook in her mother's eating-house. When her mother had died suddenly, not long after her father's death, they had decided to sell up and start afresh out West. It was while they were crossing the plains that her husband had taken ill with stomach pains.

After burying her husband, in a simple ceremony, Beth asked Flynn if he knew of anyone who wanted a cook. Flynn said yes, he did. Two months later Beth Fielding became Mrs Pat Flynn.

Pat Flynn's only other wish, that day, was to see George Tobias ride into view, but the young, black giant had just broken camp a long way away, with his squaw Nahita, in North Dakota.

## NINE

Grant was now President. None of the promises made to the Indians, allowing them to live on their own lands, were being kept. Indian villages were raided by new settlers and the occupants slaughtered. When the Indians retaliated, the army was called in, and more killings ensued. A certain General Custer was well to the fore when it came to camp raids. Many of the Indians were herded on to reservations and those who preferred to roam the plains, were hunted and slaughtered.

The two observers watched such a chase. Three young bucks crossed in front of them with soldiers in hot pursuit. Four rifles cracked simultaneously. The fleeing horses crumpled in their stride. The young Indians hit the ground. Two lay stunned. One rose, crawling on all fours to escape. The horse-soldiers drew their cutlasses as they approached their wounded quarry. Their laughter mingled with the agonized cries of the youths as they slashed mercilessly. The sun reflected on the flashing steel.

The two watchers sat immobile on their horses, witnessing the slaughter of three young lives. The fallen youths lay still with blood pumping out of neck and head wounds. The third Indian, still instinctively twisting and turning, despite blood pouring from a shoulder wound, found himself directly in the path of one of the horses. A sword flashed once more in the sun and the severed head of the Indian was trampled by the soldiers' horses. A roar went up from the cavalrymen at their accomplishment. Then they turned and rode away, leaving the slaughtered Indians to rot in the sun.

Tobias and Nahita, emerged from their cover, nudged their horses forward and slowly rode over to the slain Indians. The first two had died from a number of wounds to the head and neck. The third had died instantly after being decapitated. Tobias sat comfortably astride his horse despite its nervousness at the smell of blood. He watched as Nahita wove her pony around the remains of the youths. Her face immobile, flushed with red. Nahita turned to look behind her. 'Tobias,' she warned, anxiety in her voice as she pointed to a group of riders advancing towards them from the Black Hills. As they neared, their colourful dress identified them as Indian warriors. Tobias wheeled his horse to face them, sitting solidly, one hand resting close to his holster. He was an imposing sight, this giant Negro, dressed in buckskins. Nahita had positioned herself away from Tobias. A safety measure, when danger threatened, to ensure that one of them had a chance to survive should any confrontation prove hostile.

A party of twenty Indian warriors stopped and circled them. The leader, a young warrior – a crazed look about him – gave orders. Then he turned to Nahita, speaking rapidly in Sioux. She replied and pointed in the direction the cavalrymen had taken. The leader made off in pursuit, his band following closely in his wake. Tobias and Nahita followed at a distance. The sound of rifle fire echoed back to them. The whoops of the warriors mixed with the sound of the shots. Tobias extended his arm, stopping his squaw from spurring forward.

'Wait,' Tobias spoke in Sioux. He had

learned a great deal of the ways and language of Nahita. They had been together now for nearly a year. They had travelled the plains, avoiding towns and nomadic bands of Indians. She had taught him well and he had been an avid pupil. In return he had improved her knowledge of the white-eyes' way of life.

The shooting suddenly stopped. Tobias moved closer to see the Indians milling about. Two of the soldiers lay on the ground, like rag dolls. The other two were rapidly disappearing in the distance. As Nahita stopped silently beside him, they watched the Indian leader scalp the fallen soldiers. He then remounted his pony and the group turned back in the direction from which they had come. Tobias moved forward a few paces, distancing himself from a nervous Nahita. She knew who the Indian leader was. It was Crazy Horse. The cavalry had been hunting him for ages but with no success. The Indian party stopped. Crazy Horse advanced alone, the two scalps, tied to his waist-band, still dripping blood.

'Who is he?' He spoke to Nahita.

'Ask me. I'll tell you,' Tobias butted in, surprising the Indian with his knowledge of the Sioux tongue.

Crazy Horse turned to him and lifted his spear threateningly. Tobias's hand darted to his pistol, his eyes locked with the Indian's. He knew he was going to test him. Crazy Horse raised his spear. A blood-curdling shout flew from his lips. Tobias drew and shot. The bullet hit the lance, cutting it in half. The war party echoed its surprise at the speed and accuracy of the man. The gun seemed to have jumped into his hand and fired. Nobody was more surprised than Crazy Horse to find himself still alive. He had heard through the drum talk and the smoke language about the black warrior, who was travelling over the Dakota plains with the daughter of Big Eagle.

Crazy Horse raised his hand as his warriors moved forward aggressively. He then spoke to Tobias. 'You have come far. Word has travelled before you. We have heard of you and your magic gun. All that they say is true. If you wish to join the tribes gathering under Sitting Bull to fight the horse-soldiers, you come to Black Hills when you are ready.' With that he rode away with his men, stopping only to collect the bodies of the three young Indians.

Tobias knew, as they rode away, that they were fighting a lost cause.

'What do we do?' asked Nahita.

'We go on,' Tobias answered as he replaced his gun. He had to find a town. He needed ammunition and provisions. They needed money as well. The money Pat Flynn had given him was getting low.

Journeying on, they neared a fort. The sentry on guard watched them approaching. Tobias did not look up as a party of men came riding out, a sergeant at their head. On seeing the pair, they came their way.

'Whoa there,' the sergeant called. 'Did you see an Indian party as you travelled in?'

'No,' Tobias replied, curtly.

'Where are you headed?'

'The nearest town we can find,' said Tobias.

'What's a Negro doing with an Indian squaw?' Again, the sergeant questioned.

'We met after her tribe had been slaughtered by a cavalry patrol.'

'You're talking out of turn, black boy. We don't slaughter people,' the sergeant defended his men. Tobias decided that if he kept the patrol leader talking Crazy Horse could make good his escape.

'We saw four of your men kill three Indian youths and they had no weapons to defend themselves. What would you call that Sergeant?'

The sergeant's temper was getting the better of him at the contempt in Tobias's voice. 'If you saw that you must have seen the Indian war party chase my men. You could find yourself in trouble, holding back information.'

'No, Sergeant, it's you who could be in trouble, allowing your men to ride about killing innocent people. Whether they are Indian or black you have no right. And if you want to kill this black man and his squaw by all means try. You won't be the first to die trying.' The black face stared defiantly at the sergeant.

Only the fact that he had orders to go after a band of marauding Indians prevented the sergeant from arresting Tobias and taking him back to the fort. 'We will meet again,' was his parting shot, as he marshalled his patrol and set off in search of Crazy Horse. Tobias watched them leave before setting off again.

They came to some railway lines and followed them. A town came into view. 'Welcome to Buffalo' the sign read. The town of Buffalo was, like its name suggested, a stop-over town for buffalo hunters. They met there and went out in groups with their wagons. This was where the skins were

154

bought, treated and then sold and trans-
ported by rail. Buffalo were getting scarce,
however, and cattle were now being shipped
in to provide food for the army and the
Indians on the reservations, which were
cropping up all over the place.

Many Indians were living and hiding in
the Black Hills. Instead of fighting amongst
themselves they were now joining forces.
Word had it that very soon they would rise
under the great chief Sitting Bull and drive
the white men from the plains. The threat
did not seem to worry the townsfolk of
Buffalo. In the main street, a preacher was
telling the people to live in peace and make
a heaven on earth and that all people were
equal no matter what colour or creed.
Tobias stopped to listen before entering the
store. The Negro and the Indian woman
entered together. Nahita made her way to
the counter selling women's wear and asked
for some under-garments, while Tobias
went across to where he could purchase the
ammunition and provisions they needed.

'You squaws don't wear drawers, do you?'
The word 'squaw' turned Tobias round, just
in time to see a young man attempting to lift
Nahita's skirt. She backed away but the man
behind her pushed her forward into the

arms of her tormentor. Nahita's hands came up and she pushed him, unexpectedly, in the chest, knocking him back. 'Why you filthy Indian.' His fist drew back to strike her as the knife flew between them, burying itself in the post, alongside of him.

'Leave her alone.' Tobias spoke quietly to Nahita's tormentor.

'Who are you?' The young man turned to face Tobias. He eyed him up and down, and continued, 'Do you know who I am?' His hands dropped to his crossed guns, which were both tied low on his hips. 'Do you want to die?' He stared at Tobias, looking for fear. The black man met his stare, eyes expressionless. People in the store moved clear of both men.

'Leave it, Kid.' The man who had pushed Nahita from behind spoke, 'We don't want any trouble from the marshal. You know he doesn't like shootings in town.'

Tobias's eyes did not leave the man in front of him. He watched him fight his inner fury. His fingers were twitching. Tobias knew that when they stopped he would go for his gun. Then Tobias would kill him.

'What's your name, nigger?' He spoke again, a sign, now, of indecision. Tobias did not answer. He just stood silent, looking at his challenger. He saw a young man attired in black. Not a big man but a man, he suspected, who felt big because he was quick on the draw. How fast he was did not worry Tobias because he knew he could beat him. It was the consequences of such an act that concerned him. What would this town's folk's reaction he?

The door to the store opened. The heavy tread of footsteps broke the silence. 'OK Montana, break it up. Get out of here, pronto. I won't warn you again. If you cause any more trouble in my town, I will lock you up.'

The young man in black turned to confront the stockily built man. The star on his chest told Tobias that this was the town's marshal. In his hands was a short-barrelled shot-gun. It was held on a strap which was draped over his shoulders and it was pointing at Montana. Tobias watched the young man relax and smile

'I wouldn't have killed him here, Marshal. I would have taken him out of town and done that. I know you don't approve of shootings in town.'

'What's causing the ruckus?'

'I was just seeing if the squaw wore drawers, when he saw fit to throw knife at

157

me. I was only defending myself.'

'Did you try to kill him?' the marshal asked Tobias.

'If I had wanted to kill him he would be dead now, Marshal.' Tobias gestured to Nahita, as he added, 'Get what you want and we'll be on our way.' He pulled his knife from the post and slipped it back in his boot.

'I want you and your squaw out of my town as soon as you have bought your goods. That goes for you, too, Montana.'

'You can't order me out of town because of a squaw and a nigger.'

The marshal's shot-gun came up as Montana protested. 'Do what you like outside of town but inside of it you do as I say.'

'What do I do Marshal if he wants to play with his gun outside of town? Do I wait for you to come and save me? Or do I save myself?' Tobias had paid his bill and was pushing past the marshal.

'This is the Montana Kid. Probably the fastest gun in the territory. I will keep him in town and give you an hour's start. After that it is up to you.'

'What would you do if he insulted your woman?' Tobias stood and waited for an answer.

'Probably kill him.'

'Then so, will I.' The black giant turned to the Montana Kid. 'I will be outside of town, waiting by the loading pens. Is that far enough away from town, Marshal?'

The door shut behind them as Tobias led Nahita outside. They mounted and went in the direction of the cattle pens, north of town. The marshal watched the broad back of George Tobias ride away and then addressed Montana. 'Well, Kid, something tells me that you have met a man who doesn't frighten easy.'

The Montana Kid checked his guns. 'Come on,' he signalled to his partner, ignoring the marshal's sarcastic tone, as he made to follow Tobias, on foot. The marshal strolled behind them, the shot-gun swinging at his side. The Montana Kid broadcast to passers-by that he was about to 'kill a nigger'. He welcomed an audience. Montana had already made a name for himself in Buffalo. He had arrived in town with a cattle drive and had got himself involved with a local bully and had shot him. Marshal Stokes had put him in jail but had had to release him when witnesses said that the killing had been in self-defence. Montana soon acquired a name as a fast gun and had re-enforced it in another shooting incident, again with witnesses. The marshal had then warned him that if he did it one more time, he would jail him for sure. Nobody was allowed to shoot it out in town. This was Marshal Stokes's law and he spent his time watchfully discouraging arguments that tended to get out of hand. He accepted that this was not always possible but relied on his shot-gun to persuade potential combatants to take their troubles 'out of town'.

The Montana Kid arrived at the cattle pens with a large number of the town's inhabitants following him. He was taken aback to see Tobias calmly standing waiting for him. His squaw was sitting on her horse, holding the reins of his mount, as if she was waiting to ride away with him. Doubt entered his mind, something that had never happened before. Tobias strode forward, stopping ten feet from him.

'You can apologize to my woman and then we will ride away. All will be settled. You don't have to die.' The words were spoken quietly, without malice.

A few of the townsfolk heard his words. Some sniggered and there were mutters of, 'The nigger's afraid' and, 'Don't apologize to an Indian'.

His partner's words, 'Take him, Kid,' were

the last Montana heard. His right hand went down for his gun. He knew it was there but he never touched it. He heard the bang and felt the pain in his stomach as he fell backwards. His legs would not hold him. He saw the giant standing over him, his gun pointing at him. He found himself fouling his britches as his eyes closed and he fell into darkness.

'OK break it up. The shooting's over.' Marshal Stokes' voice broke the stunned silence. 'And you. Move on now. I don't want any other fast guns coming here, looking to try you out. My town ain't no shooting gallery.'

Tobias nodded and walked over to Nahita.

'By the way, boy, what's your name?'

Tobias mounted and turned in the saddle as he nudged his horse forward. 'I'm a "nigger", Marshal, who can shoot a gun.'

A cattle train sounded its whistle as it came into view. The onlookers turned their attention to the big man who was stepping down from the slowing train, shouting, 'Tobias. Good to see you son.' Pat Flynn jumped down and ran towards his dumbstruck friend. Tobias gripped Pat's extended hand and was literally pulled from his mount and hugged affectionately by the big Irishman. Pat Flynn stepped back. 'You're looking good, son. And how is Nahita?' He turned to look at her. She was still as pretty and as quiet as ever. She sat looking at Flynn. Had he come to take Tobias away from her? The strong bond was still there between them.

'We were just leaving, Pat. The marshal is another one of those creatures who doesn't seem to like Negroes and Indians.'

Marshal Stokes watched the reunion and wondered what they could have in common. It was obvious to him that they were friends. He interrupted their conversation when he heard Tobias's last remark. 'I'm Stokes, the marshal of Buffalo, can I welcome you to our town? And you, sir, are...?'

'Pat Flynn's the name. I own the F and T ranch, Silver City way. These are my cattle – correction – our cattle,' he answered, pointing to Tobias, 'We have a contract with the Army and the Bureau of Indian Affairs to supply them with beef. This is my first delivery so I came along with two of my men to make sure that things went well.' As he spoke, two men stepped from the train. Pat Flynn shouted orders to them and left them to unload the cattle. He addressed the marshal again. 'I want to stay in town for a few days, with Mr Tobias, to discuss some business plans. I'm sure you won't mind, Marshal.'

Tobias was surprised at the way Pat Flynn talked about contracts and business plans. Flynn had told him that he was part-owner of the ranch but Tobias had left, not thinking about his half-interest.

'Mr Tobias can stay in town with you, Mr Flynn, but I don't want any trouble. I won't tolerate any shooting in town.' With that, the marshal spun on his heel and, ordering the spectators to disperse, he made his way into town, as the body of the Montana Kid was removed to the undertaker's.

'Well, Tobias, what are your plans for the future?' Before he could answer, Flynn continued, 'I have got myself a wife now and I'm to be a father later in the year. I have put money in silver mining, which is doing well. The ranch is making money and half of it is yours.' He paused for a moment and a note of sadness came into his voice. 'And Elly Morgan left her ranch to us both. We have more than we ever dreamed of. Come home son and try and settle.' George Tobias looked at his old friend. Flynn's hand gripped his arm. 'I'm off to Chicago in a few days. Why not come with me? They want silver and, if the price is right, a good deal could be reached.'

Nahita stood listening. She heard and

understood all that Flynn had said. She had a great love for Tobias and watched him as he fought to make up his mind. If she was not here, she knew that he would have gone back with Flynn to try and settle again.

'I would like to visit my people in the Black Hills. You go on long journey with your great friend, Flynn. I will see Tobias, here in Buffalo, at the next new moon. Then we go to live with Flynn. Soon, plains run red with Indian and white man's blood. Then we must learn to live together.'

Nahita mounted her pony and left, heading in the direction of the Black Hills. Tobias watched her go. She had made up his mind for him. Nahita understood him well and he accepted that she needed to visit her people before the onslaught they both knew was coming. Their relationship was so close that often they did not even need to speak. She would go but Tobias knew that she would be there, waiting for him, when he came back for her.

Flynn was overjoyed to be with Tobias. He showed him the FT brand on the cattle. Then he told him more about his wife and how they had met and about the silver mine and how Wallace, the miner, had asked for his backing and of the mine's success.

Tobias let Flynn talk. It was something he was good at.

Three days later the two friends were on the train to Chicago. Tobias sat in the new clothes that Flynn had bought him. They both spoke of the past year and of the heartache of losing Elly Morgan and Mano. Further conversation ranged over the ranches, the silver mines and how their lives had changed. Pat Flynn was now looking forward to a bright future and said so. They were going to see a Mr Hans Graffe, a German silversmith, who had come to America and built up a well-established business which was held in great esteem.

They were met at the Chicago railway station by an associate of Mr Graffe and taken to an hotel. Flynn and Tobias were made comfortable and after a meal and rest they were picked up and taken to Hans Graffe's house for a drink and a chance to talk business. Hans Graffe was a big man and spoke with a heavy accent. A man, in his late forties, he had arrived in America, with his wife, twenty years previously. Things had gone well for this astute business man. His designs of silver brooches, rings and other trinkets had sold well and enabled him to increase his staff and premises. With his ideas and skilled workforce his business had prospered. He was looking now for a better silver and that coming out of Silver City, was the high quality he needed. If they could agree on a price, he was hoping to do a deal with Pat Flynn and his partners.

The meeting and discussions went well and talk turned to more pleasurable interests. It transpired that the German was a member of the local gun club and he invited Flynn and Tobias to be his guests for a few days, so that they could visit several venues that were coming up shortly.

The next day Hans Graffe escorted his two guests to the gun club, where they were introduced to the silversmith's business friends. Jocular comments were made about them being 'Western cowboys' and they were asked if they would like to show off their shooting prowess. It transpired that the group of friends enjoyed a side bet in friendly competition but both Flynn and Tobias declined their invitation to participate, preferring to watch. The members did not argue. They loaded their guns and took it in turns to show off their marksmanship. Hans Graffe with typical German efficiency won the bet, then asked Flynn if he would like to show them how well a man from out

West could fare against his counterparts from the East. 'As a friendly gesture,' was how he put it.

'All right then,' said Pat.

'Rifles or pistols?' the German asked eagerly, obviously excited at the opportunity for further competition.

'I will have the rifle; Tobias will oblige you with pistols.' Flynn selected a rifle after inspecting several. Tobias chose a Navy Colt like his own.

'Visitors and guests first, Mr Flynn,' said Hans Graffe, standing to one side, New targets were set up in the shape of a bull's-eye. The men stood round quietly as Flynn stood tall; his action slow and precise, his rifle steady. The first shot took out the centre bull followed, accurately, by the remaining shots. Graffe was the first to shake Flynn's hand. His friends were just as enthusiastic. Tobias was forgotten for the moment. He stood quietly by as the members fussed over Flynn. Graffe turned to apologize to him.

'I'm sorry, Mr Tobias, perhaps I might get my revenge on you, with my pistol, which I am best at.'

'Would you care to go first, then?' Tobias asked amiably.

Hans Graffe accepted the challenge. He

prided himself in his ability at pistol-shooting. He put his five shots circling the edge of the centre bull. Tobias, gun in hand, looked at his target, eyes unblinking, his massive presence dwarfing all around him. His shooting was a replica of Pat Flynn's. The five shots were dead-centre. This was pistol-shooting at its very best. The same warm-hearted response came from Graffe and his associates. Tobias was overwhelmed by it.

Flynn and Tobias accepted Graffe's invitation to stay on for a business convention, which was to be held later in the month. Tobias agreed, as long as he could get back in time for his meeting with Nahita. The two friends were enjoying their stay in Chicago and were made most welcome wherever they went. The day of the business convention arrived. Graffe was full of enthusiasm. If things went well a lot of business would come his way. After the meal he had promised everybody a big surprise, which he was keeping secret. The dinner went well. The men retired to the bar. The dining-room was cleared and a lot of activity was going on inside. Nobody was allowed into the room till Graffe's surprise was ready.

The drinking and talking was interrupted by a man who asked for Graffe. They spoke in hushed tones then Graffe excused himself and left urgently only to return later looking troubled. He sat down beside Flynn.

'What's wrong, Mr Graffe, is there a problem?'

'My surprise for the evening has been ruined,' he said.

'Is there anything I can do?' Flynn offered.

'Only if you can box,' Graffe replied. 'I arranged a heavyweight boxing match for tonight but one of the fighters is injured and it's too late to find a replacement. I feel so ridiculous, after all the secrecy. I will have to tell everybody now.' He rose as he spoke.

'Wait.' Pat Flynn got up with him, signalling to Tobias to follow them. Flynn led them out to the bar. 'Is the other fighter here, now?' he asked.

'Yes,' Graffe nodded. 'I've given him the money I promised him because he was ready to fight. But why all the interest, Mr Flynn? I must announce my little surprise is off.'

Flynn turned to Tobias. 'Do you fancy fighting here, tonight, and saving Mr Graffe's bacon? He can't get a replacement in time. It's the least we can do. If you won't fight him, I will.'

'Sergeant, you're too old now and anyway

you're married. If you go back with a black eye your wife will shout at you,' grinned Tobias. 'I will box him. How serious is it to be?' he asked Graffe.

'See how it goes. I left the arrangements in the hands of a local man, who fixed these fights. They can be rough because a lot of money gets involved. Maybe it would be better if I cancelled it. Are you experienced enough, Mr Tobias?'

'I'll fight him. If it gets out of hand you can stop it.'

Graffe was pleased with the idea of a fight taking place and went away to arrange things. The fight was duly announced to Graffe's business friends who were surprised and pleased.

The man who was to fight Tobias was named Bull Jackson. He was squat of build with a broad, hairy chest and shoulders, a shaven head and short, thick muscular arms. A mutter went through the audience as he arrived and was introduced. Several of them had seen or had heard of him. The word spread quickly about his prowess as a fighter. Hard, cruel, rough, unbeaten were just some of the attributes he engendered. Tobias appeared with Flynn, as usual, in close attendance, fussing and rubbing and talking. Sweat glistened on his muscular body. Flynn had warmed him up, ready.

The ring, which had been erected, was strong structurally and built of two-ropes depth. Jackson watched Tobias as he entered the ring, with no sign of concern. Tobias was taller than him, longer-armed and more lithesome in limb. Money was being put on Jackson; not many were backing Tobias. Odds of three to one encouraged some of the doubters to part with their money.

The local match-maker was acting as referee. The gloves were donned and after a quick word from the referee, 'to protect themselves at all times', the fight was on. Flynn's last words were, as usual, 'Watch him. Don't underrate him, son', as Tobias stepped forward, moving easily. Jackson's massive arms were held up high. His huge bald dome seemed to have shrunk into his shoulders. He stood in the middle of the ring as Tobias moved round, seeking an opening for his jabbing left. The only thing he was able to hit was his shaven head, an action that seemed to have no effect on him at all. Towards the end of the first round as Tobias's jab made contact, Jackson's right parried it, then seized it in an iron grip. He held it tightly, then threw a left hook which hit Tobias in the stomach. Only his speed of foot saved him as the same punch whistled past his head. At the shout of 'Time', Tobias turned to go back to his corner. Jackson stepped after him and delivered a tremendous punch to his kidneys. Tobias fell to his knees. The acting referee got between the two men. He pushed Jackson away casually, then turned to assist Flynn, who was lifting Tobias to his feet. Flynn protested to the referee but was told to tell his man 'to protect himself at all times'.

Flynn worked on Tobias during the interval, rubbing his back. 'It's going to get rough, son. This man is not playing games.'

Tobias acknowledged the warning. He had never been hit so hard. Only his fitness enabled him to continue. At the shout of 'Time', Tobias expected Jackson to rush him but he did not. It was the same procedure: Tobias jabbing, trying to open him up. 'Time', the shout came again. Tobias turned to his corner, then turned back in time to see Jackson, who was following him, in the act of throwing a punch. Tobias stepped to one side and met him with a right cross. All his weight was behind it. The punch hit Jackson on the point of his jaw. His eyes glazed as he fell flat on his face, unconscious. Jackson's trainer jumped, protesting, into the ring. Tobias, ignoring him, walked to his corner. The referee came over. Flynn, stopped his outburst, by saying, 'He should have defended himself at all times. Didn't you tell him?' Jackson was pulled to his feet but was in no fit state to continue. The people who had bet on Jackson were paying up – in silence and disbelief.

Graffe was the first to shake the victor's hand, clutching a bundle of money, which he had won on Tobias. 'You are two remarkable men. It is surely an honour to have met you and to call you friends,' he said.

The festivities and discussion about the fight went on till late. Graffe and a number of the business men offered to back Tobias against any known fighter in America. Flynn said they would think about it but that he and Tobias would be leaving the next day as he wanted to get home to his wife and Tobias had an appointment in Buffalo.

The following morning, at the station, Graffe presented both men with a package saying, 'Take these, in appreciation for what you did for me last night.' He shook their hands, warmly, and waved them goodbye.

# TEN

Once settled on board the train, Tobias opened his package. Inside were two silver pistols, with a waist belt and a shoulder holster. Tobias picked them up, balancing both of them for weight.

'They are perfect, Pat. They must have cost him a fortune.'

Flynn picked up his package. He knew what it was before he opened it. The silver plates on the stock shone, as he stripped off the wrapping. It was a perfectly balanced repeating-rifle. A note fell from the wrapping. *Thanks, again. Hans Graffe.* Flynn looked at Tobias, who was grinning from ear to ear. His strong white teeth shone in his brown face.

'It's good to see you smiling again, son. Things will get better from now on, I can feel it.'

Tobias nodded. 'I hope so, Pat. I hope so.' They parcelled up their gifts and settled in their seats, ignoring the curious glances from their fellow passengers. Tobias thought of Nahita and if she would be in Buffalo when he got there.

'By the way, did I tell you that that was the best punch I ever saw you throw?' Flynn broke into his thoughts.

'I know and that was the only way I could have got him,' Tobias replied.

Both men made themselves comfortable for the long journey back to Buffalo. Flynn hoped that things would improve, in the future, for his young friend. The train rattled and swayed across the Dakota plains. Through the window a few roaming buffalo could be observed. What had once been a spectacle, when thousands could be seen, was now becoming a very rare sight. Some-one on the train took a few shots at them. The crack of the rifle fire roused the dozing Flynn. He sat upright in his seat. 'It's OK Pat. Somebody's aiming shots at the buffalo but not being very successful.'

The communicating door opened and two men, with rifles, came through. 'We might get one from the conductor's coach,' one of them said as they hurriedly pushed their way through, ignoring the protests from the buffeted passengers, as the swaying coach caused them to stagger.

Shots were heard from the back of the

train. Then silence. The two men came back in. This time both had pistols in their hands and bandannas up around their faces. 'Put all your money and other valuables in this bag. Anyone with guns, throw them in the aisle. We don't want no heroes,' one threatened, as he put the black, cloth bag in front of each passenger, his pistol pointing, menacingly. Coming to Tobias, the bag in his hand, he demanded, 'Any money? In the bag.' Tobias did as he was bidden. So did Flynn. The wrapped packages were ignored. 'Throw your guns in the aisle.' Tobias took his pistol from his holster and tossed it in the aisle and sat back, patiently. Pat Flynn followed suit.

The hold-up was done with great speed and efficiency. One of the men hollered through into the next coach and the shouted reply was soon followed by the arrival of four men. Two of them were carrying bags full of money and valuables whilst the others carried the confiscated firearms. They cleared the floor in Flynn's coach and all six men entered the conductor's coach shutting the door behind them. The train began to slow down and Flynn looked through the window to see a rider, with six horses in tow, gaining on the slowing train.

One passenger got up out of his seat with a gun in his hand. He tried the door to the conductor's coach. It was locked. He fired at the lock and tried the door again. Four shots answered him. The bullets punched four holes through the wooden panels of the door before entering his body. He crumpled to the floor. People screamed and ducked down, fearing more reprisals. Flynn and Tobias were watching the rider, with the bunch of horses, drawing closer to the back of the train. One by one the hold-up team jumped expertly into the saddle. When the last of them had left the train, Tobias pushed his way through the panicking passengers to the rear door, leading into the other coach. He took the gun from the lifeless fingers of the dead man and opened the door at the rear of the train. Standing on the narrow, railed platform Tobias could see that the seven raiders were rapidly moving out of pistol range. He took careful aim and fired the four remaining shots that were in the gun. Three of the riders fell. The other four spurred on their horses as the train ground to a standstill. People were beginning to climb down, cautiously, from the train, shouting to one another.

Tobias re-entered the coach to find Flynn

untying the conductor who had been bound and gagged. Leaving him to explain what had happened, they walked to where the three hold-up men lay. They were all dead. Two of the bags, with valuables in them, were nearby. Other travellers began to venture over to where Flynn and Tobias were. Flynn organized a number of them to carry the bodies back to the train, where they were duly laid, alongside the murdered passenger, in the conductor's coach.

Tobias, with a handful of passengers, walked the line and found their confiscated guns, scattered about. Retrieving them, they returned and reboarded the train. When all the passengers were back in their seats the train set off again on its way to Buffalo. The valuables that had been stolen were claimed by their owners and conversation was solely concerning the raid and how the black man had partly foiled it.

The train entered Buffalo with its whistle screeching. People were gathering, to enquire about the noise that was being created. As the train ground to a halt, passengers were shouting to friends who were waiting for them. The marshal was there, alerted by the strident whistle, his shot-gun cradled across his forearm. Flynn waved him over.

The marshal hurried down the station platform to join them.

'What's happened?' he asked Flynn.

'We were held up. Seven men were involved. Three were shot by Tobias but four made their getaway,' Flynn replied, as he showed the bodies to Marshal Stokes.

'Who's the other man?' asked Stokes, after he had identified the three men as members of the Ashton gang. They were known bank robbers, who now seemed to have turned their attentions to robbing trains. 'Your friend could be in for some money. There's a Wanted poster on these three.' He turned to Tobias, 'You should go in for bounty hunting, the way you handle that gun of yours.' The marshal looked again at the dead passenger but could not identify him. Then he accompanied the two friends into town, pushing a way through the townsfolk, who strained to get a glimpse of the black gunman. After escorting them to their hotel, Stokes left them saying he had a town to run. Tobias sat with Flynn in their hotel room, discussing the hold-up and the reward money.

'It will come in handy, Pat,' Tobias chuckled, 'I could get used to this. What did Stokes say? A thousand dollar reward?'

Flynn studied Tobias to check if he was serious about becoming a bounty hunter. A knock on the door interrupted their conversation.

'Come in,' Flynn shouted. A stranger entered the room, stopping dead in his tracks at the sight of the two big men, one black, one white. Their visitor, a tall thin man, stood frozen just inside the room. He took off his hat and clutched it in long, nervous fingers.

'My name is Dobbs. John P. Dobbs. I make and repair watches, here, in Buffalo.' He held out a hand, which was gripped by Flynn, who was amazed at the strength in the long, slim fingers. Then, shaking hands with Tobias, Dobbs coughed as he sought for the right words to account for his intrusion. 'I understand you gentlemen were on the train that came in today. My brother was the passenger who was killed. He was coming to visit me for a while. Would you mind telling me what happened?'

'All we can say is that we were held up and our valuables taken at gun point. There was little we could do,' Flynn told him. 'They locked the door after telling us to stay seated but your brother got a gun from somewhere and fired into the lock. They returned his fire and he died on the spot. I'm sure

180

Marshal Stokes has already told you this. Tobias, here, shot the three gang members who were brought back in the train. The marshal said that they were part of the Ashton gang.' Flynn waited for his reaction.

'How long will you be staying in Buffalo?' he blurted out.

Tobias answered this time. 'We will probably leave tomorrow. Why do you ask Mr Dobbs?'

'I will pay one thousand dollars for each of my brother's killers.'

Before he could say any more, Flynn cut in, 'We are not interested in any bounty money or any revenge hunt. We have our business to run. We're sorry about your loss, Mr Dobbs, but we can't help you.'

The watchmaker turned and left the room, a sorry figure. His bid for revenge had been rejected. An hour later, he saw Flynn and Tobias walk past his shop. Pat Flynn had his rifle in his hand; Tobias's new silver pistol was tied low on his hip and, under his jacket, there was now a shoulder holster, in which was the twin of the one on his hip. Both men headed for the loading pens and their meeting with Nahita. Passing the Silver Dollar saloon, four, drunken cavalrymen came bursting through the batwing doors, and careered into Pat Flynn and Tobias.

'Well, look who we have here? Where's your squaw, black man?' The three sergeant stripes and the voice alerted Tobias to the trouble that was to come. People stopped to watch as the sergeant's strident remarks reached them. Flynn stopped Tobias from turning, pulling him along. The sergeant and his three comrades followed behind them.

'Hey, Indian lover.'

Tobias broke away from Flynn and faced his tormentor. 'What do you want, Sergeant? An excuse to do some killing?'

The sergeant stopped at the sight of Tobias facing him, his coat open, a pistol tied down at his side, his hand close to it and – slightly to the right of him – a man pointing a rifle. He knew now his words were going to get him killed.

'If you draw that pistol, I'll blow you to hell and back,' Marshal Stokes's voice broke in. The sergeant knew that his life had just been saved by the lawman, who stepped between himself and the black gunman. Stokes's shotgun was levelled at Tobias. 'I've told you I don't like shooting in my town.'

'Let's see how good he is without a gun, Marshal,' one of the soldiers butted in. 'Let him fight with his fists like a man.' This caused the sergeant to step forward, now that the gun threat had gone. His dignity was still smarting from the last time they had met. Tobias had humiliated him in front of his men. He had a reputation as a fighter and now was his chance to regain his self-respect. 'Take your gun off and I'll show you how to fight.'

Flynn lowered his rifle. 'We don't want any trouble, Marshal,' he said, adding quietly to Tobias, 'Let it go, son.'

Flynn wondered why the sergeant had caused this trouble. Then it dawned on him that this was the sergeant of the patrol that had had a run-in earlier with Tobias and Nahita.

The marshal lowered his shot-gun as the sergeant continued his aggressive attitude. Stokes did not like Tobias because the towns-folk, here in Buffalo, said it was the black gunman who had saved the train and had also got rid of the Montana Kid, something *he* had not done. He had seen and had enjoyed watching the sergeant fight in a number of bar-room brawls, which he had stopped only when they had got out of hand. He was confident of the sergeant's ability.

'Gunmen don't fight, Sergeant. They have no need to.' Stokes's voice was loud enough to carry to the crowd, milling about. Tobias took his gun and handed it to Flynn. The one under his coat, he left in its holster.

'Excuse me, Marshal.' Tobias pushed him to one side. The sergeant stepped up to face him. He took his hat off and threw it at Tobias, throwing a punch at the same time. It was a move that had paid off a number of times in the past. His punch hit thin air and a left hook brought him up short. He staggered back. Then he regained his balance. His senses cleared. The black man stood in front of him, his left hand extended. In it was the sergeant's hat. He watched Tobias. Suddenly the hat was beating his face and head. Then it stopped. The arm was extended again. The hat was dropped as he reached for it and his tormentor hit him in the stomach. He rushed forward trying to catch Tobias unawares. A knee to the face straightened him up. His nose crunched sickeningly. He expected Tobias to attack him again and instinctively covered his face in defence. Tobias stood off, watching him. He peered between his raised arms. His three friends watched him. He looked round at the ring of people, then his gaze sought his tormentor. The eyes in the black face looked coldly at him. His arms were down by his side. The sergeant roared his defiance and, stepping forward, he aimed a vicious kick at Tobias's groin. A gasp came from the crowd as Tobias caught the aimed foot, inches from the chosen target. The cavalryman hopped on one foot as the Negro's right fist exploded on his jaw. His head jolted back. Then another punch hit him. Then another. They were hurting punches but not hard enough to put him out of his agony. A vicious blow added more damage to his bleeding, broken nose. Tobias released his foot as he fell and lay still, then faced the other three cavalrymen. His eyes challenged each man, daring any of them to step forward and finish what their sergeant had started and failed, so miserably, to complete. Each one turned away, silently refusing his challenge. Marshal Stokes broke up the crowd as Tobias went on his way with Pat Flynn. He knew Nahita would be arriving soon and he had no intention of keeping her waiting.

The crowd had thinned considerably, having lost interest in the combatants, once the fighting was over. Just one man watched with interest as he stood in the doorway of his shop. John P. Dobbs was still hopeful that he might have found an avenger for his brother's death.

# ELEVEN

Nahita halted her pony and wheeled it round so that she could take one last look down into the narrow climb she had just made. Dusty stones were still rattling downhill. Part of her wished to tumble down with them but she knew she would be just as fragmented if she stayed in the Black Hills. Her visit had been a strange one, confirming her deepest dread yet strengthening her spirit and love for Tobias.

It had been easy for her to find her people. She knew that she was being watched even as she crossed the scrubby edge of the plains and began to climb the lower slopes. Once over the first rise, Nahita was confronted by two scouts who flanked her pony and escorted her, without a word spoken, through the hills to an encampment of Sioux Indians.

The women in the camp welcomed her and plied her with questions as she refreshed herself. She knew that word of her arrival and subsequent identity would mean a summons to a meeting with the elders.

That evening she was called to the tent of the medicine man. A circle of elders surrounded the wizened, bedecked Indian who beckoned Nahita to the centre of the circle. She followed his instructions meekly, with downcast eyes, and sat cross-legged and immobile as he intoned incantations over her.

Then came the questions. The elders wanted confirmation and explanation of the stories they had already heard about Nahita, the daughter of Chief Big Eagle and her friend the Black Warrior. Patiently she recounted the experiences that she and Tobias had endured: how she was disgraced by the white men, cared for by Tobias and subsequently avenged by their deaths. She spoke of the sufferings shared by herself and the Black Warrior, of the killing of his friends – Elly Morgan and Mano – followed by their acts of revenge. They asked about Tobias – his strength, his skills, his bravery – and listened intently to her replies. 'Where is he, this Black Warrior who gave you back your honour?' she was asked.

'He has gone on a long journey with his friend. I will see him again at the next full moon.'

'Why are you here, Nahita, daughter of Big Eagle?'

Nahita looked around at the faces that encircled her. She could not give any a name but in each she saw her people, her family. Then she spoke. 'The strings that bind my heart are twofold. They have been fashioned through love and respect for all that I have been taught by my people and all that I have learnt from another, the one you call the Black Warrior. Many times has my way been strewn with bad things but I have been given help and strength to survive. But the path I travel is a troubled one. The thongs round my heart tighten. I long for the spirit of my people to strengthen me.' Nahita bowed her head in silence.

'Our lands are indeed troubled, daughter of Big Eagle. But the Great Spirit has joined our tribes together and soon we will rid ourselves of the bad things that are with us. Your stay will be honoured by the women and children and your spirit will be strengthened.'

Nahita was dismissed and left the tent. She made her way through the camp and climbed heavily up the dusty slope till she reached the top of the ridge. A clean, fresh breeze whipped across her face and through her hair. Pulling herself upright she made her way carefully, bracing herself against the gusting strength of the wind. Along the ridge she travelled, sensing the rocky earth beneath her feet, smelling the air around her. Listening, always attentive. Reaching the highest peak she sat down and, wrapping her arms around her bent knees, she lowered her head and closed her eyes.

'Daughter of Big Eagle, open your heart.' The voice floated to her on the breeze. Nahita remained motionless. 'Daughter of Big Eagle, loosen the thongs.' Again the words came to her, calm and clear. This time she knew the direction of the voice and, turning her head, she looked back. The buffalo head-dress of the medicine man identified him and she dropped her knees sideways in order to face him. He motioned for her to remain still and halted a few feet from her, standing firm on the ridge with the wind blowing around him. The breeze disturbed her hair but the medicine man's dress and stance was as granite.

'Your name is known to your people. The stories of your trials and courage give strength and hope to them. These gifts they honour. Your heart is heavy with longing for us and our ways but your path is not our path. Had it been so you would have had no tales of strength or hope to bring us. You are

189

far from your father's resting place but near to his heart. I will leave you with him. Return to the camp refreshed, Nahita, daughter of Big Eagle.' With that, he turned and made his way back along the ridge, disappearing into the gloom.

Nahita stayed motionless, silhouetted against the evening sky. Slowly the air around her was filled with the sounds of the earth. The sound of wind through leafy branches, the trickle of a stream, the distant rush of a waterfall. The landscape around her lightened and she found herself in a sunny glade, long favoured in her childhood. Through the glade ran a dancing stream, on its way down from rocky heights, pushed strongly by the rush of water from a cascading waterfall. Facing her, across the stream stood her father, Chief Big Eagle.

He spoke but his lips did not move.

'Nahita, my daughter, you are not lost. The strings that bind your heart are true. All that I have taught you is so. That others do not know this is heavy for their hearts, not yours. Tobias is strong in his heart and he has learnt much from you. Together you will follow the hard path ahead. Look always into your hearts. You will find the true spirit there.'

Questions rose to Nahita's lips but she had no need to voice them.

Her father continued, 'All will not go well with our people. There will be much killing, for the white eyes do not yet understand that *they* belong to the earth. They believe the *earth* belongs to them. For our people to survive they must learn the ways of the white eyes. How else can you train a pony unless you know its ways? Learn their ways, Nahita, but use them with your own spirit or all is truly lost.'

Nahita closed her eyes and sank to the ground. She lay motionless breathing with the earth. As calmness enveloped her once more she raised herself to find her father standing next to her and in his arms lay her spirit son.

'Yes, my daughter, your child is here with me, waiting. He will return to you one day.' With that he extended his arms towards her. Nahita stretched out her hands to take the baby and, as she took him in her arms, the scene changed and she found herself once again on the ridge, hugging her knees. She curled up, behind the ridge-top and slept. Her sleep was filled with good dreams of her childhood. She awoke refreshed and of good spirit.

The weeks passed quickly and were pleasant ones for Nahita. She could move freely amongst her people enjoying the company of the women and children as she had done when her father was alive. Though she was still a *woman* in their eyes, the elders and braves treated her with respect and if she wanted solitude she was allowed to wander off into the hills without an escort. This she did from time to time, if only to be alone to think on what her father had said. She wished that she could see him again but knew that this was not something she could ask for. She found a small waterfall, away from the camp. It was secluded and Nahita loved to strip and bathe beneath its invigorating waters. Her cares would be washed away in their passing and the waters would sing to her their songs of the earth. As the time drew closer for her to return to Buffalo, she began to regret that she could not spend longer with her people.

One warm morning, she had finished her bathing and was dressing herself when she heard an exchange of familiar Indian calls. She sprang behind a rock and scanned the heights around the waterfall. Time passed, with Nahita as still as the stone she crouched behind. She recalled her old skills. Waiting was no problem to her. She controlled her breathing and listened intently for unfamiliar sounds. The splash of pony hooves into the basin at the foot of the waterfall and the fall of displaced rock either side of her told Nahita that she was surrounded. She stepped clear of her hiding place to face Crazy Horse astride his stomping pony. Either side of her, on foot, appeared his two scouts. As he recognized her his face clouded over.

'What are you doing here, daughter of Big Eagle and where is the Black Warrior?' Nahita's explanation did nothing to clear the scowl on his face. He was disappointed to hear that the Black Warrior was not with her and, in his eyes, Indian women were never allowed to wander away from the settlement without protection, not even the daughter of a chief.

She declined his offer of a pony and set off in the direction of the encampment. Crazy Horse watched the lithe, handsome Indian woman loping ahead with her hair streaming behind her. She was strong of limb and sure of foot and brimming with vitality. Such a woman interested him very much. Arriving at the camp, Crazy Horse spent the day talking with the elders. As the women prepared the evening meal they teased Nahita about her morning encounter with Crazy Horse. Perhaps he had heard of her exploits and had come to look for her? Perhaps he would take her for his woman?

Nahita shrugged off their banter though what they were suggesting bothered her. When her tasks were completed she took herself into the hillside, within view of the camp-fires but away from the hustle and bustle. What was it her father had said? That her son would be returned to her. Surely he meant also the son of Tobias? If what the women were suggesting was true, then Crazy Horse could be interested in her. What then of Tobias? Crazy Horse had been very angry to find that he was not in the camp. She knew he respected his prowess as a fighter and possibly saw him as an ally in their future skirmishes with the white eyes. But how safe would Tobias be? She foresaw an enemy within. She suspected that Crazy Horse envied the Black Warrior's prowess, and now, if he was showing an interest in her, Tobias would be faced with added problems. It was time for her to go. She had come to a decision and, as she made her way back through the wigwams, a shadow looked across her path. It was Crazy Horse.

'Where have you been, Nahita, daughter of Big Eagle? We have been looking for you. You will join the elders. I will go with you.'

Nahita's heart sank as she followed the young chief into the centre of the camp, where the medicine man was waiting. He took her to her own tent and she was surprised to find that none of the elders were waiting there. They sat facing each other in silence for a while. Then the old man spoke.

'Chief Crazy Horse has asked for you to become his woman. He agrees that I should speak to you as your father. I know what is in your heart and that you are happy to be here, at this time, with your people. You have our respect. What you say, will be.'

Nahita looked past the medicine man and thought she saw her father, holding her son, standing in the shadows of the wigwam. 'I am honoured to have the respect of my people and the interest of one such as the great Chief Crazy Horse. You know that I have talked with my father. I think that he is here with us now and what I say he will hear. He told me that the son I lost, will be returned to me. The son who has the Black Warrior for a father.'

The medicine man nodded. 'What else did Chief Big Eagle say?'

Nahita looked to the shadows before answering. 'We must learn the ways of the white eyes yet use them with our spirit, or else all will be truly lost.'

'So be it, daughter of Big Eagle. I will tell Chief Crazy Horse of the honour you feel and that you must be with the father of your child. You must return and continue, as your father has commanded, under the strong arm of the Black Warrior.'

He rose and left Nahita alone. She looked around her. The wigwam was empty. She would depart at first light. Leaving the tent, she wandered to where the women were grouped. She savoured their laughter and banter and felt a sadness to be leaving them. That night's sleep was a restless one and Nahita was glad to see the light dawning. She was soon astride her pony and stepping out of the camp. The guards nodded as she passed, for her leaving was known to them. Passing through the wigwams, without a backwards glance, she set off towards the sloping hills. The climb was gradual and she was well clear of the encampment before she dismounted to lead her pony slowly upwards. Zig-zagging along an invisible path which steepened with every step, she patiently and expertly made her way. The air was still and she drew deep gulps as she wended uphill. Nearing the first of many rises she stopped to rest her pony and for the first time looked back over the scattered encampment. Figures were beginning to stir. Soon they would all be awake following their daily chores. It looked so peaceful, so right. If only it could stay that way. Nahita sighed and turned to continue her travels. Her sigh turned to a gasp as she saw that she was not alone. Crazy Horse stood before her.

'Why do you sigh, Nahita? Does it not fill your heart with pride to see our people, so? Soon they will be free to camp wherever they wish and life will return to how it used to be. I, Crazy Horse, will make it so.' He stood proudly arrogant, young and convinced of his invincibility.

'My task is to return to Tobias. I am sad to leave my people,' Nahita explained.

'I know. I have spoken with the medicine man. If you should lose your Black Warrior you will come to me. I have spoken.' With that he led the way down the other side of the ridge ahead of Nahita and escorted her to the heights bordering the plains that skirted Buffalo.

There he stopped and standing with his back to the plains he stepped closer so that she could feel his breath on her face. 'Remember what I have said, Nahita, daughter of Big Eagle.' She held his gaze, in silence. He dropped his eyes, mounted his pony and abruptly circling, he began his journey back to the Sioux encampment.

Nahita waited till he was out of sight before dropping back, well down, over the ridge. It would be better to spend the night in the hills she had decided, before making her way into Buffalo the next day. She settled down for the night. The sky was clear. The moon was full. The stars were scattered and brilliant. Sleep came easily and soon she would be with Tobias, once again.

Nahita's visit had strengthened her spirit. She no longer felt pulled between her people and Tobias. The medicine man and the spiritual visit to her father had wiped away any doubts she had had.

It was late in the afternoon when Nahita entered Buffalo and headed for the loading pens, where she was to meet Tobias. She saw him standing with Pat Flynn and made her way across the pens towards them. Tobias saw her approaching, her hair tied back. He had never seen her look so beautiful. Her eyes sparkled in her face. She was caught in his strong arms as her pony halted by him. The breath was crushed from her body. His lips brushed hers lightly as she melted into his embrace.

Embarrassed, Pat Flynn stood to one side, watching the happy reunion. Only his loud cough broke them apart. After welcoming Nahita back, Flynn told Tobias to go and put Nahita's pony with his own in the stables till the next day, while he went to book the train journey back to Silver City. Pat left the young lovers still locked together and made his way to the station, where he booked three seats and accommodation for their horses. As Flynn walked back from the station, in the direction of his hotel, he saw four riders make their way to the stables, leave their horses and walk to a Chinese eating-house. They stopped outside and the eldest of them spoke to one, who appeared to be the youngest, and handed him something, which he pocketed before walking on, into town.

Flynn watched the youngster, trying to place him. He knew that he had seen him before somewhere. Flynn carried on to his hotel, stopping in the doorway, to watch the young cowboy enter a shop opposite. The name above it said JOHN P. DOBBS. Flynn slowly made his way across to the watch-maker's premises. He looked through the window and saw Dobbs taking an object from the young man. Pat Flynn walked through the door to hear the young cowboy say something about the watch being left to him by his father and that he had to sell it because he needed the money. J.P. Dobbs was examining the watch. His hand went under the counter. It came out holding a pistol. Flynn acted instinctively, raising his rifle. The face of the young man had finally registered. It was the face of the rider who had raced alongside the train, with the horses, when it was held up. John P. Dobbs pointed his pistol as Flynn levelled his rifle.

'Hold him there, Mr Flynn. This is my brother's watch. I gave it to him.' The watchmaker came from behind the counter. Flynn took the hold-up man's gun from his holster and put it in his belt. Dobbs cocked the hammer of his gun back and shoved it, angrily, to the outlaw's head. 'Tell me where the rest of your gang is or I will kill you here and now.'

'There's no need for that, Mr Dobbs,' Flynn butted in. 'I know where they are. Let's get this one down to the marshal's office and then we will see what he wants to do.' Pat Flynn took hold of the young man and, with Dobbs in tow, escorted him to the marshal's office. Marshal Stokes was surprised by the intrusion of Flynn and his little entourage.

'What's going on?' he queried, as they entered his office. Flynn left it to Dobbs to explain.

'This man brought a watch in to sell and I recognized it as my brother's. It is solid gold and worth a deal of money. Mr Flynn came in and helped me to arrest him and bring him here.'

Stokes looked at Flynn for confirmation of Dobbs's story, to which the Irishman added, 'I recognized him as the man who brought up the Ashton gang's horses when they held up the train. The rest of the gang is in the Chinese eating-house on the outskirts of town.'

'What's your name?' Stokes asked, as he examined his Wanted posters, with the help of one of his deputies.

'Tex Young. I haven't got a poster out on me. I've only just joined Ashton and his gang.'

Stokes tossed the cell keys to his deputy. 'Lock him up,' he directed. With that, the marshal picked up his shot-gun, broke it open and checked if it was fully loaded. Then he put the strap on his shoulder.

'I want you two to act as deputies,' he told Flynn and Dobbs.

'Wait a minute,' Flynn said. 'Let's not go charging in shooting. We'll have to organize this.' He could imagine the damage the shot-gun would create in the Chinese diner. 'We'll go in first and get a seat near the gang. When you come in, we will cover you as you enter.' Stokes agreed.

Flynn left with Dobbs who was eager to avenge his brother's death. Stokes watched them go. He wondered where the big Negro was. He knew of Ashton's reputation and that if he saw any danger of getting caught he would shoot and not worry whom he killed.

Dobbs entered the diner behind Flynn. He was determined to help in any way he could. If Marshal Stokes had not wanted him as acting deputy he would have come along anyway. Flynn ordered coffee for them both. The three men, under observation, sat by the window. Between mouthfuls of food, one of them kept looking up the street. The two acting lawmen sat two tables away. Flynn's rifle was on his knee. Dobbs sat opposite him, his hands restless under the table. From time to time he would feel nervously in his inside pocket, checking for his pistol.

The three hold-up men had watched Flynn come in with his rifle. Their hands had gone to their guns, expecting trouble, alert to any sudden danger, but Flynn had ignored them, which eased their worries.

The Chinese waiter started clearing the tables as people left. Soon, only Flynn and Dobbs were left with the men by the window. The waiter stood between the tables as Stokes entered the dining-room. Ashton, who had been watching the street, had seen the marshal's approach. His gun was out as Stokes entered. He fired low, hitting Stokes in the thigh. As Stokes fell, both of his shotgun barrels exploded. Their murderous pellets hit one of Ashton's partners, as he stood up, his body taking both barrels. Ashton made for the door but the Chinaman stood between Flynn and his quarry, spoiling his aim. Dobbs pulled out his gun and shot the third member of the gang, as he stumbled over his blasted, bleeding partner. Ashton made it to the street, and headed towards the stable.

Pat Flynn's rifle came up and fired. The window shattered as Flynn's bullet went through it on its way to its target. His shot hit Ashton at the side of his head. Ashton's legs carried him several yards and then he fell and lay still, with blood running from the hole behind his ear.

The Chinese waiter remained standing, still as a statue, while the bullets flew around him. When the commotion ceased, he sat down and looked first at the wounded marshal – who was cursing under his breath and holding his leg – and then at the two dead men. One had been nearly cut in half by the shotgun, the other had been shot by the watchmaker. Dobbs was still standing by Flynn, who had lowered his rifle now and was giving orders to the nosy people, as they pushed to get in the diner, past the cursing Stokes, who was trying to rise.

Tobias and Nahita were in the stable on the upper floor. Tobias had paid the stable-man ten dollars for some privacy. They heard the shooting but they ignored it. Tonight, Nahita knew that the seed of her son was to be sown. She lay still as the pleasure ran through her body. Then she slept in the safe arms of her Black Warrior.

At dawn, the sound of the ostler, going about his chores, woke them up. The appearance of Tobias and Nahita did not seem to bother the stable-hand. He stood and watched them leave the stable and cross the loading pens, as they strode together in the direction of the hotel, where Pat Flynn had slept the night alone.

Flynn was up and ordering breakfast when Tobias entered the hotel with Nahita. The dishevelled pair caused a few stares and comments but they were silenced when Flynn welcomed them both and took them upstairs to his room, to freshen up, after their night together in the stables. Pat Flynn did not question Tobias about it.

'You missed out on the excitement, last night,' Flynn told him.

'I didn't, you know,' Tobias answered, with a big grin.

Flynn laughed with him, causing Nahita to blush.

'We had visitors: Ashton came in with his men. Apparently they didn't get a lot of money in the hold-up. What they did get they lost when you shot his three men. They came in to sell a very expensive watch. Fortunately I recognized the young man as the wrangler who was in charge of the getaway horses. It turned out that the watch they were trying to sell, was Dobbs's brother's which he recognized when the wrangler took it in to his shop. We caught him and then

Ashton and the rest of his gang shot it out with me and Dobbs along with the marshal. We killed the three of them.'

'Can't I leave you for a minute, Sergeant?' Tobias feigned shock.

Nahita rejoined the two men after cleaning the straw from her clothes and hair. Tobias took her in his arms and kissed her.

'Pat,' he said, 'we want you to know that we have decided to return to Silver City with you, to settle down.'

'Fine. Fine, son. This is how I always wanted it to be.'

The publishers hope that this book has given you enjoyable reading. Large Print Books are especially designed to be as easy to see and hold as possible. If you wish a complete list of our books please ask at your local library or write directly to:

**Dales Large Print Books**
Magna House, Long Preston,
Skipton, North Yorkshire.
BD23 4ND

This Large Print Book, for people
who cannot read normal print,
is published under the auspices of

## THE ULVERSCROFT FOUNDATION

... we hope you have enjoyed this book.
Please think for a moment about those
who have worse eyesight than you ...
and are unable to even read or enjoy
Large Print without great difficulty.

You can help them by sending a
donation, large or small, to:

**The Ulverscroft Foundation,
1, The Green, Bradgate Road,
Anstey, Leicestershire, LE7 7FU,
England.**
or request a copy of our brochure for
more details.

The Foundation will use all donations
to assist those people who are visually
impaired and need special attention
with medical research, diagnosis
and treatment.

Thank you very much for your help.